365

WAYS TO CONNECT WITH YOUR KIDS

NO MATTER WHAT THEIR AGE [OR YOURS]

BY CHARLENE ANN BAUMBICH

CAREER
PRESS

FRANKLIN LAKES, NJ

365 WAYS TO CONNECT WITH YOUR KIDS
Editing and typesetting by John J. O'Sullivan
Cover design by Cheryl Finbow
Printed in the U.S.A. by Book-mart Press

To order this title, please call toll-free 1-800-CAREER-1 (NJ and Canada: 201-848-0310) to order using VISA or MasterCard, or for further information on books from Career Press.

CAREER
PRESS

The Career Press, Inc., 3 Tice Road, PO Box 687,
Franklin Lakes, NJ 07417
www.careerpress.com

Library of Congress Cataloging-in-Publication Data

Baumbich, Charlene Ann, 1945-
    365 ways to connect with your kids : no matter what their age
(or yours)/ by Baumbich, Charlene Ann.
        p. cm.
    Includes index.
    ISBN 1-56414-480-1 (pbk.)
    1. Parent and child—Miscellanea. 2. Parenting—Miscellanea. I. Title
Three hundred sixty-five ways to connect with your kids. II. Title.

HQ755.85 .B37 2001
306.874—dc21   00-050055

DEDICATION

This book is dedicated to my sons, Bret Lee Haskins and Brian George Baumbich.

There has never been a day when I haven't been thankful and blessed to be connected with you. Even though some of those days were, and continue to be, crazed, feisty, slam-dunked, lonesome, mouth-gapingly astounding, and filled with "duh!," many more were, and continue to be, showered with laughter, awe, applause, pride, and spirited kindred hearts—long distance though much of this may be. I would not trade one moment of any of these days; their unending stories are the mortar and grace that hold us together, connected forever.

Thanks for loving me, even when I'm acting horrid. Thanks for teaching me, by your witness in the world, how a man becomes a man. Thanks for surprises, muddy faces, humbling moments, innocent eyes, high fives, and savory meals you've cooked for me. Thanks for being rowdy rascals and helping me learn about road burns, dating (from the Mars side), wrestling, skateboarding, career success, contentment, and adult-to-adult, parent-child relationships. Thanks for cheering *me* on in all of my endeavors, including this one.

But especially thanks for being no more or nor less than exactly who you each are, for even now when you're mid-life men, you are still my sons, my boys, my babies.

Thank you. Thank you.

Peace and grins, Mom XO

ACKNOWLEDGMENTS

In the beginning of this project there was a guy named Mike Lewis who asked me if I'd be interested in writing this book, to which I replied thanks but no thanks. And then, The Book—which had, unbeknownst to me, lodged itself in me somewhere—started talking to me. I couldn't stop thinking about it. It was stuck to me like a booger on the end of a finger. So finally I phoned the guy named Mike Lewis. Next thing you know, we were working on The Book. Without Mike Lewis, this book would not exist. Not only did he take a leap of faith by believing I could write this book, but he ushered and cheered me and The Book along the entire way. And now I wish to cheer him, King Boogiemaster. Hip Hip Hooray! Hip Hip Hooray! Hip Hip Hooray for King Boogiemaster! (You, Dear Reader, now know that Mike, the editor, and I, a writer, became friends somewhere along the way when calling him King Boogiemaster became a term of endearment.) Thanks, Mike.

After the beginning I began talking about this project with friends and acquaintances. They not only resonated with the idea but began telling me their stories. It was then that The Book told me it wanted more voices than my own. Through conversations and e-mails with friends, acquaintances, and strangers on airplanes, the stories were collected. This book is rich because of the combined voices of more than 70 people who have contributed. Many have bylines; others simply desired to have the story told, sans names. Thank you to each person who listened to the call of The Book. You have helped fill The Book's belly with deep, important, and fun substance. Charlene and The Book thank you. (I'm sure the readers will, too.) Also thanks to those whose stories didn't make the final cut. All the stories were great and touched me, but there was only room for so many.

Of course, my husband George has had to put up not only with The Book, but with me, and that was no small task, especially when I was working on The Book. This meant I was not working on The Dinner, The Laundry, or The Cleaning. And not only did George pick up the slack in these areas, he did so without grumbling, loving me all the while. Thank you, George, for loving me, picking up slack, and staying connected—through thick and thin, dirty and clean, silence and words, and decades of child rearing. Your Honey Bunny loves you.

I have already thanked my children in the dedication. But thanks again guys. XOXOXOXOXO

CONTENTS

Introduction

I am the mother of two grown "boys"—ages 35 and 29. By God's grace, sheer willpower, sleep-deprived decisions, wide-eyed victories, horrific blunders, tons of laughter, truckloads of forgiveness, countless moments of letting go, and skillions of celebrations for the small pleasures in life, they are happy, out-of-the-house, self-supporting, balanced, and productive people. (I've stopped typing for a moment to celebrate, yet again!)

We enjoy each other's company; well, most of the time. (We are human, after all.) We love each other profusely, in spite of our differences. We delight in sharing our stories, whether they're good, bad, or dubious. We surprise one another via long distance phone calls, road trips, and jet rides. Although neither I nor my immediate family members are taking trips to the moon, curing diseases, or winning "Mother-" or "Kids-of-the-Year" awards, we wallow in the blessed knowledge that we truly like one another. We know that we are available during crisis modes, mundane minutia, and flat out "yahoos," because we desire to be so.

Genuine parent/child bonding is a cooperative, honest, sometimes slam-dunking, often fun-inducing, and occasionally gut-punching rollercoaster ride where both parent and child are strapped in together side by side. Touching. Holding their breath. Yelping— sometimes concurrently—with glee, questions, or dissatisfaction. Being who they *really* are and accepting the same in one another. Connected by a simultaneous give-and-take, yet each is free to fly when they need to. (And of course we all must every now and then.)

Oh sure, parents of young children have to be "in charge," much of the time; otherwise our children would drown in their own unmet diaper needs, be perpetually crabby for lack of naps and stay out all night at age 14. But child rearing is not one sided. In my humble yet bold opinion, "child rearing" is not even an exemplary phrase for parenting as it leads one to believe the efforts and giving are all from the parent to the child when there is more, oh so much more, like the spontaneity, enthusiasm and lessons our children have to share with us!

Since I wrote *Don't Miss Your Kids! (they'll be gone before you know it)*, I've had occasion to speak to thousands of parents around the country. Way too many parents are stressed out and filled with fear. It seems they live in a perpetual state of full alert, watching for "Caution," "Danger," and "Parental Error" messages. They worry more about how they're doing as parents rather than being there for their children. Sounds crazy, you say? But think about it: When all your attention is on your parenting and the "dangers of the world," your eyes are not on that child. And your children have so much to offer, show, and teach you. There is energy, spiritual zest, and a true connection in realizing that the parent/child bond is a two-way exchange. It is haughty and a great waste of opportunity to believe otherwise.

The ideas, thoughts, meditations, activities, humor, examples, and occasional rantings in this book are my endeavor—and that of other parents as well—to help you connect with your children in a positive, fun, thought-provoking, rewarding way for both of you. It will also hopefully encourage you to more fully enjoy your own life apart from your kids. They are, for the most part, presented in story form in an attempt to not only tell you how to connect, but to *show* you, through example, what has worked for those who have connected with their children—whether from the parent or child's perspective.

No matter what the age of your child (even if they are now adults) or yourself, it is never too late to try something new or revive something old and meaningful. Some thoughts may seem obvious; others may seem silly. A few dip from the deep well of honor; some may make you groan. Some will touch and inspire your soul while others...well they might add a bit of sparkle to your lives, causing you to spontaneously scream, "aha!"

All of them, however, are intended to spread good will, self-esteem, joy, satisfaction, a moment to exhale, and hope to everyone involved. They are intended to lighten your load while strengthening your relationships. They are each an attempt to help get you connected with your child, your child connected with him or herself, and then in turn for that assured person to be ever ready to raise the next generation with zest, joy, honor, and blessings.

Read them one a day or read the book straight through and then start over again. Put sticky tabs on entries you want to remember—especially three or four years from now when your kids have reached "that" phase. Stay with one that speaks to your heart until you get it implemented in your family. Or keep moving along trying them until something—*something*—makes a difference. The point is: *Use* this book like the instructional, inspirational spring board, entertaining, life preserver, and breath of hope it is intended to be.

The 365 Ways to Connect With Your Kids

1. Begin to let go

It is never too early or too late to begin to let go. I remember holding Bret, my eldest son, in my arms for the first time and realizing that I would, ultimately, have to lie him down. It felt so unsafe—and almost scary—to let go of that fragile, precious, hope-filled baby and to trust he would be okay when I wasn't looking. Now, almost suddenly, he's 35 years old...and I have that same sensation each time I wave goodbye at the airport.

Each of us deserves the right to become who we are, apart from the wants, desires, needs, and eyes of another. In fact, we cannot fully know ourselves until that freedom arrives. And so it is perhaps the utmost gift of connection—to child *and* parent—when we begin to let go so that one day we can truly know the child who has fully discovered him- or herself.

2. Look full in your child's face

I once heard a 70-year-old father say that none of his children had brown eyes. I heard this...as I was looking directly into the brown eyes of his adult son—and he only had two children to keep track of.

What does it say about us and what have we communicated to our child if we have not studied our child's face? What unspoken sign, clue, or message might we miss if we don't look for it? Answers are often revealed in the corner of a mouth, the wrinkle of an eyebrow, or the placement of freckles.

Much like a baseline medical test, there is important information to be gained by the study of a resting face so that we might notice when it changes...for the better, the worse, or the dubious.

3. LAUGH AT YOURSELF

Let's face it, we all have our "duh" moments. What a gift we can give to our child by allowing them to see that we do have those moments. And yes, we can laugh, gain perspective, and move on. Perhaps the suicide rate in our teens wouldn't be so high if they knew we allowed for and modeled laughter in the midst of our foibles, humbleness in revealing our own shortcomings, and joy in the everyday ability to freely embrace life's adventures and mishaps with both arms.

4. EAT DESSERT FIRST!

When I'm speaking at all-day parenting conferences, one of the things that always makes me grin is watching the women eat their boxed lunches or hit the food facilities. These moms are in charge of their kids and their own health. They know better about nutrition and teach the same. However, when they are out for the day, they choose the cookie over the apple, caffeine over calcium, and candy over cole slaw. However, I've never noticed a single one of them losing a tooth or contracting rickets.

Kids grow up despite the fact they hate broccoli and anything else that isn't a hot dog. Lighten up parents! Occasionally, allow the entire family to eat dessert first. Everyone will love you for it. (Besides, you've just been busted and I might just squeal to your kids if I'm given the chance.)

5. WINDFALLS

I remember receiving cards from my grandparents when I was young. Birthday, Christmas, and sometimes even Valentine's Day—the holiday prompted the action. The first thing I did, of course, was shake it to see what might fall out, hoping it was a few bucks.

As an adult myself, my father would, for *no* particular reason, occasionally send me a wad of bucks with which to "do something fun." (Sometimes the wad was little, sometimes it was big.) It was always a complete surprise. No strings attached.

The grandparents' gift came for the occasion; my father's gift created one. Whether the money resulted in ice cream or a new fountain pen, Dad gifted me with his thoughts and his wallet. But most importantly, he gifted me with his belief that I would drop my busy life just to celebrate the windfall and the knowledge he was thinking about me.

6. FACE TO FACE

What about your physical appearance is like your child's? (Notice the order there.) Stand next your child in front of a mirror and go over the details. What is the same? What is not? And what about your hands? Fingers? Knuckles? Nails? Knees?

What they will learn is not only the results of this exploration, but that you enjoy standing beside them, seeking common ground while noticing and honoring the differences.

7. TWIRL YOUR WHIRL

When I was a little girl, my mother used to keep a large chest full of dress-up clothes handy. It contained much more than clothes: The giant chest was a place for me to discover my fancy, creative, and feminine side. It was bountifully stocked with scarves, jewelry, and high-heeled shoes in which I could shuffle and wobble across the floor.

My favorite items, however, were dresses with twirly skirts. In particular, there was one beautiful number mom had procured from a rummage sale. It had a black velvet, sleeveless top that came to a point at the waist. Yards and yards of cream colored satin flowed from the bottom of the dress. I would don this Cinderella costume, then twirl and twirl until it billowed as far as it could fly. Then I'd quickly hunch down, allowing the flying fabric to settle down around me, softly brushing against my arms and sometimes my cheek. I would sit nearly holding my breath until the entire magical fabric landed.

What gift of flight, fancy, and wonder can you give your child today that might have a memory as lasting as that? Do you have one of your own? Share it with your child.

8. Divine invitations

Fear

Once while attending an estate sale, I was working my way through a closet, when what to my wondering eyes should appear but a dress almost exactly like the one from my childhood! I unhooked it from the clothes rod, held it up in front of me, stroked the satin, closed my eyes, and relived the moment. I wondered...could it be my old dress? Having no daughters or grandchildren yet and attending the sale alone, I had this overwhelming desire to pass on my memories and experience with anyone because the sensation was so powerful and tangible.

Just as I was casting my eyes around and ready to burst with wonderment, a little girl about seven years old appeared before me. I quickly checked the price tag on the dress: five bucks. "If I give you this dress," I said, "would you promise to take it home, wear it, and twirl in it?" My voice was filled with enthusiasm and I'd squatted down to show her the treasure. "I used to have one like this when I was a little girl and I can still remember it!"

In a flash, her mother had yanked her out of the room and out of the house, never to be seen again. Suddenly, I was the enemy. I was the stranger. I was the perpetrator relentlessly described on the television.

I was wounded and saddened beyond belief. I felt like a vulnerable child with a beautiful bouquet of dandelions which had been seized and thrown into the fire.

What do we, in fear or simply as a result of our busy lives, snatch away from our children, whether they're on the giving or receiving end of magic and mystical moments?

9. TOUCH THEM

Touch the top of his head, her shoulder, a hand. Don't talk. Just smile and touch. There is power in connectedness that has no message attached.

Then again, perhaps the touch *is* the most important message of all.

10. ANTICIPATION

BEDTIME

(Provided by Michael Lewis)

When you put your child to bed, tell them how excited you are about the great day they're going to have tomorrow. I started doing this with my daughter Sam by reminding her that she had school the next day, or that her friend Anton was coming over, or whatever.

Once I said it, knowing full well that the next day really was just an ordinary day, she said, "Why Daddy? Do I have school tomorrow?" And I said, "Every day can be a special day if you want it to be special. As special as you want to make it."

11. BLAH BLAH BLAH...

When my youngest son was out of the house and on his own he began a practice that was at first disturbing. (He was a smart boy to wait until then!) Sometimes in the middle of my deepest pearls of wisdom he would begin saying, "Blah blah blah," right over my words.

Well! I must say that my pride was a bit dinged. But in a rare bit of wisdom, I didn't pull rank like I might have when he was just a lad. Instead, I stopped talking and changed the subject. Of course I did my fair share of pouting after we hung up or just moved on.

After the first couple times he did this, however, I realized that this always happened during my longest and most often repeated "pearls"—which were really not pearls at all but diatribes and opinions my "baby" had not asked for.

About the fourth time it happened, I stopped short and said, "Oh. I guess I was lecturing again, huh?"

"Yes," he said, then chuckled. Enough said?

12. Signs and symbols

When I was young I collected sparkly rocks.

When my children were young they collected sparkly rocks.

As an adult I *still* collect sparkly rocks. I decorate with them now, collecting and selecting from vacations, local trips to the park, or my own roadside. I have them placed in different decorative containers around our home, even using one larger set for a cornice railing in our bathroom.

I love the fact my children can witness a parent's ability to continue to look for what shines and sparkles in life and receive the simple yet clear knowledge that it can be found.

13. Honoring the others

It is never too early (or late) to create a calendar for your child that announces all the dates you believe they should remember. Dates such as family birthdays (including the pets), parents' anniversary, other landmarks, vacations, whatever. Use stickers or photographs or pictures clipped out of magazines for younger children; even have them cull magazines to find them.

Whether they are five or 35, every child (and I still consider myself to be one) loves the feeling of giving. It is sad to have a heart filled with love for someone and then find out you've missed a special occasion—which perhaps everyone else remembered—to show them how much you care. (Or perhaps an event that *no one* else remembered!)

Watching calendars for opportunities to celebrate can help children of any age, including yourself, endure the moments that aren't so hot.

14. Be there when you are there

A friend and I meet for breakfast once a week at a local restaurant. On more than one occasion we've seen the same father there with two children. They are a beautiful brother and sister, the oldest probably not more than five the first time we saw them. Dad orders for them. He gives directives. He occasionally cuts something for them.

However, he does not look at them; his head is buried in his newspaper which is next to his plate. They do not talk or laugh, any of them. He does not engage them in any way.

In his silence he communicates volumes.

15. Be E.T.

Who can forget the image of that lovable, quirky alien reaching out his long spindly finger? The illumination in that moment of touch was cause for goose bumps.

What if you pointed your finger toward that child of yours—and I'm not talking that *wagging* finger—while engaging all your imagination, pretending to possess those same powers? What if, when you tried to imagine the magical, electrical, potent connection at the instance of touch, you literally experienced it?

Okay, so maybe you won't see the zoom of light rays and your heart won't skip a beat. But if you and your child approach this task with wonder and imagination (usually a much shorter leap for them), *something* will happen. Worst case scenario: You will have connected in a less dramatic way. But you will have connected nonetheless.

16. Birds of a feather

My friend Marlene Fenske has a way of making even bad things feel good. The day her grandson e-mailed her to tell her he'd fallen over a bush and knocked his teeth lose, she e-mailed him right back with a promise to send him a "Hurt Day" present. But most importantly—at least from an adult perspective—she connected with him at an important core level with empathy. She shared how she'd fallen on *her* face recently and needed a Hurt Day present herself.

17. Fading Moments

(Provided by Gundega Korsts)

Twilight seems to be a time for connecting. Especially summer twilight. Walking, just the two of you, parent and child. It's a magical hour for a child, and you can remember your own childhood in that twilight. For a few minutes, walking together, you are equal in the yearning beauty of a day deepening into dusk, falling into night. Both wanting the moment to go on and on and on forever. ("I don't want to come home and go to bed." Sometimes that's the voice of a moment's breathless beauty.)

You may not talk at all. But if you choose to speak, what you say may come deeper from your heart, and may be heard with more quickened-to-the-moment ears.

One summer night I had called and called for Toby to come home, until I had to go down the street to where the boys had been playing kick the can. "You must come home," I said. The reluctant captive walked with me, loudly resistant in his silence. I started talking about how I, too, love the twilight: the day deepening into dusk and on into night, when even in the dark my eyes can still see and as long as I stay out here this beautiful day will never end.

My son looked up at me, in surprise. "Oh! You understand!"

That was all we said, until we got upstairs into the lighted house and life went on.

18. FLY THE FLAG

Every year in this country we celebrate Flag Day. It is an awesome patriotic reminder and gives us cause to pause and consider what that red, white, and blue stand for.

Perhaps as well as celebrating the U.S. Flag Day, each family ought to create its own flag day. You know, one where we gather our banner of pride, fly the "family colors" and spend a moment celebrating what our family stands for. It would be called "Baumbich Day" at our home.

Challenge your kids to create the family flag. (It's okay if you join them.) Ask what symbols they believe should represent your family. What colors "feel" like your family? Tell them what you would chose. (This is good food for thought for yourself as well.) Chat and come to a consensus, settling on as few or as many as you like. Then create your family flag, large or small, made of fabric or freezer paper. Fly it on your front door or your refrigerator. But fly it.

19. WHAT IS RIGHT?

FEAR

As I type, the media has barraged us with unending visions in yet another episode of violence in our schools: Teens killing one another and then themselves. Children perpetuating crimes against their own youth. A sense of hopelessness and worry seizes parents and children alike who find themselves asking, "Why? How? What's gone wrong? Can we do something to prevent this? Can we throw away all the guns? Can we have enough metal detectors? Is my child safe outside our doors? Am I?"

My observation is this: In the midst of our questions, shock, and fear, rather than concentrating on what's *right* about our lives and helping our children to find it, we are unknowingly perpetuating what is wrong. We are not helping foster security, hope, and the knowledge that violence isn't the answer to loneliness or anxiety; we are instead—by our fretting—further feeding the frenzy.

It is time to turn off the television and plug in to our children and one another. Time to, with intent and all of our senses, link in a way that assures our caring, presence, and support. It is time to become a daily part of the answer.

20. ENTRYWAY

(Provided by Jan Limiero)

We've all heard it said, "The way to a man's heart is through his stomach." While I can't argue with that, I would have to add that the way to your child's heart is also through his or her stomach.

I vividly remember riding that big yellow bus watching the memorized scenery go by like clockwork, the same every day. The other thing I could count on being the same every day was that Mom would be waiting for my sisters and me with a snack. That snack at the kitchen table met more than just a physical need for food at a time when blood sugar levels were dropping—it met an emotional need for security as well. I could count on my mother to be there for me! "How was your day?" and "What did you do?" might have been met with a disinterested "okay" and "nuthin," but inside my heart was won.

AFTER SCHOOL SNACK:

- *1 plop of butter.*
- *1 frying pan full of Cheerios.*
- *A few of shakes of seasoning salt.*

Fry Cheerios in butter and shake with seasoning salt.

(I'm sure somewhere there's a real recipe. But it became one of those favorites that you just remember.)

---

21. ALL THAT NICE

I can amaze myself. I can be talking to clients, friends, and the guy or gal at the local grocery store and just be so incredibly nice. Real nice. I bet I've been so nice that people are walking away thinking, "I'm so glad I got to see her today."

And then I get home. Grrrrrrr.

What sometimes happens to all that nice at the end of a work day? Do we use it all up or something? Do we not value those we live with and are raising as much as we value and honor and respect our clients and co-workers and the toll booth person?

Reach down deep. Don't downshift all your nice away on the way home. And if you're staying home all day, don't save it up for when you leave.

22. BE MINE

VALENTINE'S DAY

I can still recall the thrill of Valentine's Day when I was in grammar school. Preparations actually began the week before when we began decorating our Valentine's Day boxes. Each child had to bring a shoebox or something like it in order to transform it into our own personal mail receptacle for the big party day. We slit a hole in the top big enough for cards. Then the magic began. We decorated our boxes with construction paper, bric-a-brac, crayons, and cutouts from magazines. Each of us were lost in our own world of vision. We would only stop creation of the dramatic renderings when the bell rang, the teacher told us to, or when we pronounced ourselves done, not a square inch left "unfroofrooed."

Then came the waiting and the process of discovery. Who gave us a card? What did it say? Was there hidden meaning behind the words or overt declarations of "love"?

Think back to those days of anticipation and hesitancy and keep them in mind as you present your child with *your* expression of written or demonstrated love. They have prepared the receptacle of their hearts—daily—to receive it.

23. CHECK IT OUT

(Provided by Carol Zimmerman)

Become actively interested and involved in some of the things your kids are doing with the neighborhood gang. Don't be afraid of other kids. Sometimes I go to the bike jump and ask questions about the tricks they are trying to do, and cheer them on when they want to show off. I am amazed at how easy it is to connect with your kids once you get involved with their friends.

You will be not only bridging gaps in your family, but connecting with the children who are—and will become—a stronger and stronger influence on your own child. Realize that you don't have to like sports, Pokémon cards, pets, games, or bike jumping yourself. The fact that you are interested in their activities shows that you really are interested in who they are. And that's a connection for life!

24. BE WRONG

"Anything but *that*!" you declare to this inanimate page. "*Please* don't ask me to admit I make mistakes, otherwise my child will lose confidence in me. I mean, I'm the parent, right? If I open the door to the possibility that what I'm saying or doing might be in error, then how can I ever stand on the statement, 'Because I'm the mommy (or daddy), that's why!'?"

Well the fact of the matter is that parents can stand on anything they want to because they *do* possess the position of power over younger children. But then again, one day those kids will grow up. What would you rather have them believe about you when they're old enough to analyze and test your statements on their own? That you are honest...or delusional?

25. COUNT YOUR STEPS

For different reasons throughout my life, I have occasionally counted the number of steps it takes to get from here to there.

The first time I recall doing so was playing hopscotch because the steps were actually numbered.

Then I remember pacing off the number of strides it took to get from the back door of our farmhouse to the barn. Sometimes, I tested the reliability of my last count by going through the drill again.

As an adult I have stepped off paces to help discern a room measurement, lay out a makeshift baseball diamond for my kids, and get through the instructions on an exercise video (argh).

The Challenge: Instead of counting physical steps, count the number of steps it takes to engage your child in a meaningful conversation. If it's a day's worth or you can't go the distance, commit yourself to shortening the gap.

26. Come see

My adult son phoned me on his cordless phone from Minnesota one evening. He was standing on his porch looking at the sky. He was trying to search for the comet Hale-Bopp, and he asked me where exactly it was.

On a few different occasions, I had asked him if he'd looked, found, studied, and pondered the miracles and mysteries of the comet. Although he had not, he now had seized a moment to do so. And so I switched to my cordless phone and went on my front porch. Together, yet many states apart, we gazed at the identical slice of the cosmos, the same comet, and shared the same moment of awe.

Whether gripping a hand or a phone, study the same sky.

27. What goes around...

"Ain't that purdy (sic)?" my father used to ask while he'd drape his arm around my shoulder and engage me in staring at whatever the pretty thing was. It might have been a sunset, a field of sparkling snow, a sky filled with hot air balloons, or a perfectly roasted turkey in the oven. It might have been one of thousands of things he pointed out to me throughout my lifetime. Although he knew and usually used better grammar and pronunciation than that (most of the time, although he did mispronounce many words by accident), this was no accident. It was an endearing and familiar phrase he coupled with a soft tone of voice that beckoned me to come see.

This gift of knowing my son now calls me to do the same is evidence of one of my father's great gifts to me, now passed on through the generations.

28. Out of control

By the time late afternoon rolled around, I didn't like myself very much. The day had begun on a bad note and a series of bad decisions kept it rolling.

I'd awakened that morning tired since I'd stayed up well past what I know is a reasonable time for me to go to bed. My tiredness incited carelessness and I sent a glass of orange juice splattering all over the place. By the time I got it cleaned up I was tardy for my first appointment. By early afternoon I'd started four projects and made headway on none of them because I was wired from too much caffeine and sugar during a luncheon. By late afternoon, my sugar and caffeine rush had soared, peaked, and plummeted and I was snapping at everyone. I mean, it wasn't pretty and my kids and spouse got the brunt of it.

As a parent, it quickly becomes obvious when our child's behavior has been affected by their bad choices. When we are the ones whose behavior runs amuck due to bad choices, it is time for us to fess up and admit we've made a series of them. Therein lies the opportunity to not only connect, but to teach as well. Keep in mind here, it doesn't matter how old you or your child are, even if you're 55 and he's 30!

"Jason, Daddy hasn't been behaving very well today. I am still a good person, having realized myself that it is my behavior and not my being that has run amuck, but my behavior has been naughty and I'm sorry. Daddy made a bunch of bad choices (spell them out here). I'll try to think better next time."

29. WHAT WE CAN'T FIX

INTENTIONAL DISCONNECT

Sometimes a family goes through one horrid experience after another and so was the case with this mom. But her utmost lesson arrived the day she learned she needed to *disconnect*—for the benefit of everyone. She learned, she says, "I was up against something that was not within my capability to fix and I had to let her go." Mom had to learn to let go of her daughter who was suffering from anorexia nervosa.

A twin, both girls had been born sick; they were in critical condition for weeks. Beating the odds, they pulled through the traumas of the birth process. Later, one twin had Leukemia and the other developed a large ovarian cyst which was removed. Again, they were treated and recovered. Her husband overcame cancer and recuperated from a heart attack. All these things, Mom said, were horrid and traumatic; but they were nothing compared to the development of anorexia. "It was the most death dealing, horrible thing to see a child slowly disintegrate. This child was so full of light and love...and the light went out and I was scared."

Mom pulled out the stops, sought the best treatment. But after 16 months, she found at one point she could no longer even pray. She couldn't do anything. She was killing herself trying to fix what she couldn't. "I had to let her go," she told me. "I had to let her go and die, if that's what she had to do. I made a decision to let her go. I prayed for me to be able to let go. And I did."

It was in that place of relinquishment—and awakening—that mom received a glimpse of eternity; she can describe it no other way. "You forget they are God's to begin with," she said. And then...her child regained her health. To this day, no matter what the problems with her children or life, they all look small next to eternity.

30. PEELING BACK THE LAYERS

Sometimes the challenge of getting a child to talk feels more like plucking nose hairs than the lively art of conversation. We can see that something is on our child's mind but our attempts to get him or her to sit down and chat just don't seem to work. They often sense the squeeze of an inquisition and close up.

Susan Elizabeth Phillips has a great decoy technique that she says works like a charm. When she could see or sense that one of her sons had something on their minds, she suddenly developed an overwhelming need to peel carrots, potatoes, or whatever else might need (or not) peeling. "The loss of eye contact opened things up," she said.

When her sons went off to college, she also recognized that if she wanted to be engaged in conversation with them, it didn't work to call them on her schedule to tell them what was going on. She needed to drop everything when they called to talk. Having had a child go through college, I certainly echo her wisdom. She is a wise parent, indeed.

31. You need a nap (so take one)

My youngest son is very crabby when he's tired, just like his mother. There are times when I simply say to him, "Brian, you need a nap!" to which he will reply, "No, I think *you're* the one who needs a nap!"

"No, *you're* the one who used that rotten tone of voice!"

"But you started it by saying…"

As of this writing, that child is 29 years old; these conversations have been taking place since he was about 12. And so our precious time together here on this earth goes for a spell until one of us becomes sensible, leaves the room, and—if we are truly struck by wisdom—takes a nap.

Become "sensible" before you teach and model "ridiculous."

32. THE POWER OF A WORD

As I look around my office I find myself comforted by the words of my children that adorn my office walls. Throughout their lives they have gifted me with cards. But more importantly, they have often taken the time to write a sentence or two of their own. Encouragements and declarations that not only blessed me when I first read them but which have continued to do so throughout the years.

"Sing your heart out, Mom!" came with the gift of a new CD.

"I think good things about you all the time," came on a birthday card.

"I think you're getting away from what you do best," words on a card wherein my son delivered a dose of reality and wisdom.

Oh the sustaining power of a written word that can be reread, just when we need to receive it again! This is something for us to remember as we pack our child's lunch in the morning or think about them during the day or wonder how they're doing at their new job.

I hope the annual letters my sons receive from Santa Claus (yes, that rascally Santa *still* sends them) reflecting on all their accomplishments throughout the year (as noted by himself and/or his elves' reports) are as long-term meaningful to my sons as their words are to me.

33. MOTHER MAY I?

"Mommy, will you braid my hair?"

"Daddy, will you tie my shoe?"

"Mom, can Carrie sleep over?"

"Mom, is it okay if I stay out until 10:30 tonight?"

"Dad, can I borrow the car?"

"Mom, can we have a party after graduation?"

"Good-bye you guys! See ya at spring break, okay?"

"Dad, do you think you'll cry when you walk me down the aisle?"

"Mom, can you please come help me decorate?"

Young children instinctively know they need to ask. They learn if you will answer. They live what they have learned.

34. THREEBIES

(Provided by Karin Baker)

> *Even the best ideas don't work when there is no em-powering follow-through. Good stuff happens when we do what we say we're going to.*

I had problems getting a handle on getting my 4-year-old daughter to listen to me in public. My husband, being a baseball coach, started a "Three strikes—you're out!" rule. Brooklyn, our daughter, has learned that when she does not listen to me or if she does something she is not supposed to, she gets a strike. When she receives three strikes, we leave that particular public place or event and she gets disciplined by getting a familiar privilege taken away from her.

In this same aspect, I wanted to start rewarding her for the good things she does. I did not want her to grow up thinking we only notice her when she does something wrong or disobedient towards us so I started the "Three goals—you win!" rule. Each morning, on our way to the babysitter's house, we both come up with three goals for the day. It can be anything from hanging up her own coat to telling her brother she loves him. It can be a smile at a stranger to helping set the lunch table. It just has to be three goals she wants for herself for the day.

At the end of the day when I pick her up from the sitter's house, we go over our goals and talk about the day, helping to set a mood of togetherness. Was it a good day or a bad day? Did we accomplish our goals? Did we do anything extra ordinary? It only takes the 10 to 15 minute drive home to connect and if the rest of the evening is in turmoil, I know that I have spent some quality time with her.

35. Achy breaky heart

Vicky Olivgrez told me about the day her 4-year-old son Robert was unhappy with her decision about something. He endeavored to impose a giant wad of guilt on her, so he dramatically looked up at her with a majorly pained face, then down at the floor, then back up at her again and said, "You're breakin' my heart. See it cracking and the pieces sliding to the floor?"

Pay close attention to the word pictures your child paints. Memorize those words and use them the next time you need to. They seem to have quite an effect on people.

36. Don't tell me

We sat in the gently rocking boat, fishing poles extended in front of us, each facing due south, backs turned to the nippy Canadian winds. The shrill calls of an unidentified bird echoed from a nearby island, drawing my attention away from the sounds of water licking and lapping at the sides of the metal boat. I turned my torso and head toward the call of the bird and heard dad's rain gear rustle, knowing he, too, had craned his body to pursue a peek at the living creation that could make such a distinctive noise.

Together we didn't talk. Together we watched. Together we waited, drawing so many past fishing experiences into the quickening of still togetherness.

My father died in 1998 and we will never share another fishing adventure, at least here on earth. But now, at this moment, I relive the splendid silence of them all.

Sometimes the best connections fill us when absolutely nothing is happening but proximity and stillness—which allow room for everything else that matters.

37. Hire a naturalist

(Provided by Will Kilkeary)

One of the most fascinating and enjoyable ways I have found to interrelate with my daughter is to have her take me on nature tours of the local woods. We started doing this when she was about 6 years old and continue to do so fairly often; she is now 10.

It is hard to say who benefits more from these excursions: my daughter, whose self-worth and confidence multiplies with each article of interest that she points out; or myself, as I am treated once again to the sight of a mysterious world through the unprejudiced eyes of youth. It always amazes me to experience the beauty and wonder that a child's eyes can find in things which my adult mind have relegated to the inconsequential world of the mundane.

Another lasting benefit of these excursions is that now, whenever my daughter and I walk the woods together, we seem to do so on an equal footing with both of us comfortably pointing out objects of interest or suggesting the path or direction to be taken next. Like the varied flora and fauna of the woods, we grow well together.

38. Follow my lead

When Bret was a rowdy youngster (as opposed to the rowdy mid-lifer he is today), he feared no evil. He loved adventure and people so much that he could easily disappear from my side in crowds.

One frustrated shopping day, after I'd spent far too much time keeping him lassoed, I decided to just let him think he was lost. I allowed him to go whatever direction he wanted to while I hid behind poles and dress racks so he couldn't see me when he turned around to look.

Which he never did. Look, that is.

After a good 10 minutes or so, he was moving so swiftly toward the tool section of the store that he careened into an elderly woman carrying a bag in each hand. Their impact dislodged a package from her hands and nearly knocked her over. At this point I made my whereabouts known, began to assist in picking up her items and I said to Bret, "Bret! What do you say to the nice lady?"

"You should watch where you're going," he said matter-of-factly. It was then I realized I should have led, not followed.

39. BOUNTIFUL EVIDENCE

All my years growing up I recall spending happy times thumbing through photographs of our family. I looked through all the pictures of my brother and I blowing out birthday candles or sitting on a picnic blanket, along with the various groupings of Mom, Dad, Jimmy, and I gathered around a holiday table.

I especially loved looking at old black and whites of me when I was very young. I certainly had my favorites, and I still do: Me wandering around in my little white undies, mud all over me, with a big stick in my hand, returning to the house from my latest backyard adventure. Or me, nuzzling a puppy close to my face while the other of his seven brothers and sisters were close by, cozied up to momma dog who had her head lifted, studying her baby in my arms.

Now that my parents are gone, I sometimes spend countless hours going through those photos. Mixed in with their boxes and scrapbooks of shots are photos of my growing family. Photos I've captured throughout the years and mailed off to Grandma and Grandpa, or ones they'd taken themselves of my family during visits. Each evidence and a reminder that we were being seen. Captured. Studied. Savored. Noticed.

40. THE RIGHT QUESTIONS

(Provided by Susan L. Day)

> *There is genuine connectedness, inspiration, and hilarity in realizing your child, in all innocence and inquiry, has asked one of life's deep and important questions.*

When Maggie was a highly observant 2-year-old, we took her to the local 4 H fair for her first experience on a ride. Thrilled first-time parents that we were, we plunked her into the little metal horse-drawn cart that went around in not-too-fast, not-too-big circles.

We did our duty of waving every time she came around the circle, laughing at how serious she looked. The best part, though, was when Scott lifted her out at the end. She looked up at him and asked, "Daddy, where did I go?"

41. NOTHING LEFT UNSAID

I was on the road for a speaking engagement when news came to my hotel room via a late-night phone call that my father had died. Shock. Plans. Wrenching tears. Cross-country flights. Arrangements. Memorial services. And then one uncommon decision among many tactical decisions needed to be made in the midst of the grief and activities.

Long ago, I was contracted to speak at a parenting conference...within days of my dad's service. I was tired, aching with loss, and physically drained. Would I be able to hold together and deliver a coherent message, or should I cancel and work on finding a replacement? Surely moms would understand if I chose the latter.

As I was praying for direction, the answer became clear. I just lost my father. When, if not now, would I feel how blessed it is to know, without a shadow of a doubt after someone is gone, how much you were loved. Loved in time, words, experiences, encouragement, direction, laughter, and tears. Loved, completely and unconditionally—no matter what.

And so I spoke. Yes, I spent a moment weeping before them. But I spoke of love and laughter and picnics and fishing. I spoke of words, moments of silence, and photographs. I spoke from the depths of someone who knew they were loved. I spoke from the shoes of my daddy's daughter.

Spend today thinking about what each of your actions is leaving behind.

42. CATCH A RAINBOW

I was visiting my youngest son who lives in Minnesota. While I was there, he came down the stairs from his bedroom with an

Austrian crystal dangling from a piece of fishing line. He proceeded to hang it in his living room window having just removed it from his bedroom window on another side of the house.

"No more rainbows upstairs," he said, knowing full well I would know what he was talking about. I not only knew what he was talking about but my heart rejoiced. You see, he grew up in a house full of rainbows.

When my kids were young, my brother sent me a crystal for a gift. I hung it in my sunniest window with recollections of one of my favorite movies, *Pollyanna*, in which Haley Mills was introduced to this beautiful rainbow-inducing phenomenon. Sure enough, when the sun was just right, objects that had before seemed gray and lifeless suddenly burst with magnificent color. Before long, I had dozens of the crystals in all shapes and sizes hanging across my kitchen window. I even baked rainbows into cookies when the light hit the oven door.

But there came a time of year when the sun was too high to capture them on the first floor and they had to be moved to another window elsewhere in the house. Yes, son, I know what you're talking about.

The symbolism of all these elements is something I'm glad I've passed on to my children and can still remember myself, especially when it is they who remind me.

43. Cheerleading

Get yourself some pom-poms. They're cheap and can be found in most toy stores. Or, you can make them out of strips of paper taped around the end of an empty toilet paper roll. Keep them handy and occasionally pull them out to cheer when your child does something notable—or even when he or she comes in the door after school. Or when he takes out the garbage. She helps set the table. They don't argue for more than an hour. They get home on time. He plays with his baby brother. He smiles at you, just when you needed a smile the most. She gets a good grade. He gets an okay grade but it's better than the one before that. You get the idea; it's something *right* you've noticed.

Cheering can consist of simply waving the pom-poms and jumping up and down a few times or simply saying "Yay!" Or if you're really happy about something they did, why not try writing a cheer, harking back to your high school days? Perhaps the garbage cheer of "Pack it up, take it out, *gooooooo* Jason!" You might just cheer *yourself* up along the way.

44. A GIFT OF GRACE

(Provided by Donna Turner)

> *Whether it's your child or another's, what we carefully*
> *offer from our hearts can be transforming.*

As a young girl of 11, I began volunteering at our church two or three times a week. I didn't do anything spectacular—mostly folding bulletins, putting on stamps, sorting and folding weekly newsletters. I did this alongside a 70-year-old woman named Grace Frauens. While we worked, we talked about our lives; Grace about her lifetime of teaching nursing; me about my 11-year-old life.

One afternoon, Grace invited me to lunch at her home the following Saturday. I accepted and arrangements were made. Her tiny apartment said "welcome"—from the fresh flowers in a vase to the white ironed linen cloth over a tiny table. Glass matching china held the already prepared food. To this day I still remember the red tomato filled with chicken salad on a green lettuce leaf. The tomato was accented with fresh fruit. I had never seen anything as beautiful.

I realized sometime later that this lunch invitation was the first time I had ever been formally invited to anything. As a kid from a low-rent housing development with a chaotic home life, Grace saw me as a person with possibilities. Further, she helped me see myself as a person with possibilities. What a gift of grace!

45. LESSONS ALONG THE WAY

(Provided by Kathy Stodgell)

> *Opportunities to connect, teach, learn, and serve are all around us; seize them.*

One evening my 8-year-old daughter and I were out to dinner. The waitress was sharing that an upcoming trip was going to be her family's first trip to Disney and her children's first airline ride. My daughter couldn't believe what she was hearing. "This is your first trip on an airplane?" she queried, rather incredulously. She'd been raised flying and taking trips so often she thought these adventures were as common as having toothpaste.

A few nights later, I asked my daughter to come to my volunteer job with me. We have a service in our community for the homeless; throughout the cold months and on a weekly rotation basis, a different church hosts the homeless, feeds them dinner, gives them towels and washcloths to wash up, and offers them a safe place to sleep. There are volunteers who work the actual shift and others who cook and do laundry and provide a variety of connected services. My job is to coordinate all the staff workers each week.

After our night together, I reminded my daughter of our dinner conversation at the restaurant. We had not only had a great time working together, but we then had a 25-minute conversation as to why people are homeless. These conversations were continued in her Sunday School classes. My daughter's eyes were opened up to many things: the fact that she *does* have a lucky life. As a stay-at-home mom, my daughter had never realized I don't get a salary for all of the work I do and how kids don't appreciate us doing their sheets and laundry and making lunches. And I also had *my* eyes open to what a hard, responsible worker *she* was!

Our volunteer job together proved to be more than community service, which would have been enough in itself. But together we had learned more about each other, as have all the other mothers and daughters, fathers and sons and families who had given something back to the world.

46. NEVER GROW UP

(Provided by Susan L. Day)

> *Sometimes the messiest of circumstances can be the purest of memories—for us and for our children. Don't get your knickers in a knot over dirt.*

When my kids were preschoolers (well, even now, and they're 7 and 9), they were always the first out in the puddles and the mud in the spring, and the last ones getting wet and filthy in the fall (usually dressed appropriately in grubbies, but not always). I'll never know the impact this has on my kids development, but I like to think that the time I spent with them sloshing through puddles and allowing them to enjoy a big mess, will help them be broader people.

I'll always remember two times. Once, when we were out in the puddles, a neighborhood girl (in fifth grade) stopped by to say hello. She stared at my son and daughter, stomping away, sitting in the puddle making gravel dams, then looked at me and said, "You let them do that?"

Another time, my daughter discovered that if she let the rear training wheels on her bike straddle the gutter, she could pedal away without going anywhere, and the freely spinning rear wheel would propel a huge fountain of water from the puddle back onto her little brother! They took turns, and just threw their heads back laughing hard!

47. BREAK BREAD TOGETHER

Break bread as a family. Literally. Prepare dipping cups of jelly, honey, cookie sprinkles, peanut butter, nuts, raisins, marshmallow fluff, or whatever else you can find. Mix little wads of butter with cinnamon and nutmeg, or garlic and crunched up potato chips...and on and on for a combination of tastes. Then rip a bite-size wad off an unsliced loaf and begin the dipping process. Single, double, or quadruple dip for taste experiments. "Mmmm. Yuck. Delicious!"

48. Watch this

I remember putting on plays, jumping off diving boards, doing somersaults, building tents out of blankets and crawling in, going cross-eyed, and all the while saying, "Watch this, Mom. Watch this, Dad." And they did. And I remember that they did. And they remembered what I did. Amen.

49. Ask

I just keynoted to 500 third- through fifth-graders at a Young Authors' Conference. While I was there, I was struck by their eagerness to respond to my questions, whether they simply solicited a show of hands or called for answers.

"Who was in scouting?" Hands wagged and waved. "See *me*," they seemed to say.

When I would present a short scenario, stop short of the ending and ask, "What do you think happened next?" Ideas were pealing out of all corners of the auditorium. "Isn't *that* a good one?" they wanted to know.

"I don't quite understand Pokémon. Can someone tell me what that means?" A cacophony of responses ensued! They were so anxious to teach me, share, respond, contribute.

Ask. Ask and then listen. And remember, there is a difference between inquiry and "the third degree." One feels interested and inviting; the other feels accusatory and invasive. If they don't answer, check your tone of voice and approach, then ask a more detailed question or a simpler one. But don't stop asking.

50. Day of grace

(Provided by Lori L. Gregor)

I have a 15-year-old daughter and a 17-year-old son. They are both great students and generally wonderful people. Sometimes, as with all God's children, they get overwhelmed by their lives. They have many responsibilities with homework, sports, housework, and other activities. So, when I notice that they are getting frustrated, behind on their work, or downhearted, I will on occasion, offer a "grace day."

A grace day means different things. It may mean they don't have to make their beds and do their other chores around the house. Or it may include staying home from school altogether and just resting. I think that our mental health is really important, and grace days help keep everyone a little more sane.

A grace day can't be asked for; it is an act of grace on Mom and/ or Dad's part. The grace day shows them that I see them and I value them. This also teaches them the meaning of grace in a tangible way.

51. Name that tune

"Turn that down!" we scream in frustration at music that hammers into our brains and goes against the grain of our personal taste in tunes. "I said **turn that down!**"

Rather than fight against what we don't want to hear, thereby silencing the offensive rhythms and alienating the child or teen, perhaps the better approach would be to ask them to please play a different song for a while. Maybe even invite them to sit down by the stereo and talk about other albums they like that might fit your current mood a bit better and feel like a good compromise for everyone. Let them introduce you to a new group you'll like, given the chance to hear it, instead of always having it turned down.

Or maybe you could work out a deal wherein they can continue playing their favorite music (even if you hate it) for the next five minutes (use ear plugs and a timer) but then announce that you will play your favorite just as loudly immediately following. (*That* might get the response you're hoping for!)

What matters is the difference between a short tempered dictator and a somewhat accommodating disk jockey. Which would you choose to connect with?

52. STUDY YOURSELF IN THE MIRROR

Study yourself in the mirror. Not for wrinkles or makeup corrections, mind you, but just to see what you see.

I remember seeing my teenage sons each taking their turns passing by the mirror in the foyer and giving themselves a serious study. Sometimes they'd flex and make a muscle. Sometimes they'd just grin. Sometimes they walked away looking discouraged. No matter what the results, however, I always felt like they'd taken a moment to honor their own presence in the world.

Let them see you do the same. Hopefully they'll catch a glimpse of your self approval, thereby giving them the freedom to allow for their own.

53. LESSONS FROM BADLAND

WITS END

(Provided by Sandra Duncan Holmes)

> *Even when they're bad, they can be very, very good...at dispensing life's valuable lessons. Pay attention to the bad.*
> *It speaks.*

❧

She was almost 2 years old and went far beyond terrible. She could evaporate the patience of a saint like a raindrop in a desert. She didn't sleep more than five hours a night. She *never* stopped talking. She had very strong opinions about *everything*. She was bad.

One particularly awful day, the last straw reached when I requested calmly that she refrain from trying to dress the cat in doll clothes because the cat was looking rather upset.

The toddler screamed, "No! She likes it!" I calmly explained that cats don't really like to wear clothes and when they're upset they will bite or scratch. The toddler screamed, "No, she likes it!"

I saw that poor cat was at the end of her rope and was about to attack. I tried to distract the toddler. I was rewarded by being bitten, twice—once by the cat and once by the child. Being unsure of my ability to control my temper, I sent the child to her room and while shaking my finger, said, "You are *not* to come out of your room for two minutes. Mommy is very angry that you didn't listen and *I need to calm down.*"

Mommy retreated to the kitchen table wondering what kind of a mother she is who allows a 2-year-old to reduce her to this quivering mass of anger and insecurity. Meanwhile, an angry yell down the stairwell, "You are a bad mommy! You are a bad and foolish mommy! I do not love you Mommy! I cannot love you because you are bad and foolish!"

Then came a silence followed by a quavering, wonderful 2-year-old voice: "Do you still love me oh bad and foolish mommy?" That question took me from tears to—tears of a very different sort. It was a moment that changed our relationship from a battle of wills to a learning partnership, one that endures to this day. (That child is now a 21-year-old junior at Princeton University.) I'm very proud of both my daughters. They've taught me more about how to approach life—through love—than I have ever taught them.

54. RIDE LIKE THE WIND

There is a richness in remembering what it felt like to peddle as fast as you could. To run full-out. To cross the monkey bars hand-over-hand, skipping every other rung. To pump so high on your swing you wondered if it might loop around the support beam and find yourself upside down, or if it might cut lose and take flight. To rollerskate around the corners with lightning speed and such deep lean that your fingertips grazed the floor. To jump in your brand new pair of tennis shoes and just know you launched yourself higher than you'd ever gone before.

Remember what it felt like. Stand up and pantomime the actions to your child (don't hurt yourself; remember, you're older now). Close your eyes and lose yourself to the sensations. Give them a peek into your past—and at your inner child.

55. MAKING CHOICES

Should I go to work out or to Kelly's game?

Should I mop the kitchen floor or cheer on Ben's shadowbox project?

Should I continue hand-feeding Rebecca or should I let her try herself, knowing full well I'll have to clean up the mess?

Every decision we make sends a message. Today, what—or whom—do you choose?

56. INDIVIDUALITY

INTENTIONAL DISCONNECT

(Provided by Gundega Korsts)

How do you connect with your child? First, you have to separate yourself from your child. For example, when Althaia was 4, she fell while skating and cracked a bone in her arm. This was during recess at Montessori school, and eventually I got a phone call. They didn't think she had anything like a broken bone because she wasn't crying. But, then again, she wouldn't let anyone move the arm.

I came to get her and took her to the clinic, just in case. The doctors and nurses there didn't think that was a broken bone because she wasn't crying. But, then again, she wouldn't let anyone move the arm.

The X-ray showed the fracture. A large cast on the small arm followed. On the way home, on the bus, I reflected on this sensibly brave and self-controlled child of mine and the thought came unbidden: "I'd like to be like that when I grow up."

From that moment on, this child of mine was forever a whole separate human being—admirable and complete—and not just a gift to me. And I, the adult, was forever someone who can still learn and grow.

I am deeply grateful to have experienced this so early in my life as a mother. The whole point of raising children is to let them go, and the point of family is to be and stay connected. I would not have realized on my own, without some such transforming experience, that connection requires first a separateness across which to connect, and that the separateness is a tribute to and expression of wholeness on both sides.

57. Imagine that!

My first serious friend was an imaginary one. Her name was Cellophane. I named her that because I was the only one who could see her; everyone else saw *through* her. What I remember about her the most is that she understood my every heartache and laughed at my every joke. She knew things about me that I didn't have to explain, even though, of course, I tried anyway.

If your child is suddenly befriended by someone you can't see, just go along for the ride. In fact, invite "the friend" to dinner or to tag along on errands when you're loading into your auto. Don't engage in too much conversation with that new friend, but allow your child to know, via actions and not explanations, that you are acknowledging his or her or its presence.

You might be surprised what you can learn when your child is free to speak to someone who doesn't argue back, contradict, or make fun of them. You might just learn what that child is thinking. At the very least, you will have honored your son or daughter's imagination. And who knows, your child might just grow up to be the next Stephen King or J.K. Rowling.

58. Take aim!

I was holding my breath, nearly twisting my husband's arm out of its socket, wondering why points were going on the board. I had no idea what high school wrestling was about, other than it seemed to be sucking the life out of me as I watched my son struggle to keep his left shoulder blade one inch off the mat. This was our first meet. Believe me, I still refer to them as "our" meets because I wrestled every one of those seconds, right along with him!

More than learning about wrestling, however, I saw for the first time what my son's stubborn bent was all about. And in that instant, I knew my job had not been to break it, but to help aim it. All stubbornness was channeled into that one shoulder. Strong will had gone from being his detriment to his greatest gift.

My next epiphany concerning his stubbornness came when he took flying lessons and I watched him circle the small aircraft during a safety check, making sure nothing was out of whack. It was nearly the same look on his face I'd seen a thousand times before when I wished I could have achieved my command for him to "wipe that look off his face." But at that moment—which could save lives—I wouldn't have traded the stubborn look or stubborn behavior for anything. (Nor did I want it to even crack a skosh when it came to peer pressure, and so it didn't.)

That child is an engineer. Nothing happens before its time. And what I learned was that our children are born with traits that are their gifts. Our job is not to break their stubbornness, but to aim it.

59. BABY STEPS

(Provided by Carolyn Armistead)

My daughter hates to clean her room. So during one especially difficult, whiny morning, I took a little time from my own chores to write up some directions on small scraps of paper and put them in a hat for her to choose one at a time. The rule was that she had to do what was on each slip of paper before drawing another one.

Some broke up her job for her. "Pick up all the dirty laundry and put in the hamper" or "Put all books neatly into the bookcase." Interspersed were fun, silly suggestions: "Stand on your head and say the pledge of allegiance," "Eat one Cheerio," or "Sing a lullaby to the cat."

It eased the tension for all of us, and even though her room wasn't perfectly clean by the end of the exercise, there was a definite improvement—in our spirits as well as in her room.

60. That's a time-out

All throughout America, parents are sending their children off to "the time-out chair" for a moment to perhaps, "Think that over, buddy," or "Imagine what it would be like if you didn't have a sister to punch," or "Stay there until you calm down."

I was speaking at a parenting function, relating a story I'd heard about this phenomenon and sharing how we'd missed the time-out-chair stage of our personal parenting because it wasn't "invented" until our children were grown. A lady walked up to me afterwards and said, with a very quiet voice, "My son was a real rascal and he spent a lot of time in that time-out chair. He died a few months ago and what I wish is that I'd spent more time in it with him."

61. Brain changers

Some of the loudest and most aggravating family moments take place around morning dressing rituals. Children go through strange phases of wanting to wear the same pair of pants for 29 days straight. They suddenly hate that color and can turn decidedly against anything that matches. They want to wear long-sleeved shirts in summer and not remove their coats in winter. Whatever you lay out isn't what they're in the mood for. And when they get to be teens…batten the hatches.

A friend of mine arrived at my home one day, deflated. She said she'd been fighting with her 7-year-old daughter all morning about something she either did or didn't want to wear. Mom finally realized that what her daughter looked like for a day (and it wasn't all that strange) didn't matter as much as the emotional trauma they were each enduring over fabric! When Mom changed her mind, the rocky waters calmed. Mom didn't say, "I give up." She quieted herself for a thoughtful moment, acknowledged to her daughter that she'd reconsidered the outfit (keeping parental authority) and had decided her daughter was right—that it really wasn't that bad. Mom agreed she could wear (or not wear) whatever "it" was today.

End of trauma. End of war. End of fighting over dumb stuff.

62. WHEELS OF FORTUNE

We have a photo of our year-old son sitting atop a short, stuffed, purple elephant with wheels on it. We watched as he learned, with our prompting and assistance, how to scoot it along the floor.

I remember running until I was out of breath, helping our son try to learn to balance on a two wheeler bicycle. I recall holding my breath as I rode shotgun while he learned to drive.

Now I simply enjoy riding alongside him in his truck. I love clinging to him when he invites me to go for a motorcycle ride: Parent and child seeing life up close and personal. Leisurely. Wind to our faces and our lives connected. Reaping the rewards of time well invested.

What are *you* investing in today? Perhaps it's time to take a moment and plant a seed, envisioning the day when you, too, can just go along for the ride.

63. BAGGING EXPECTATIONS

(Provided by Sandy Koropp)

For me, connections are sometimes about relaxed expectations. My kids are tiny (4 years, 2 1/2 years, 8 months) but I can't help but have a few expectations—perfect pictures in my mind for the precious Santa visit or ballet class. I hope I've learned by now that it's much more fun for us all if I stay as open-minded as I can and watch for spontaneous sparkle.

Take a crimson afternoon last fall, perfect for an afternoon at the arboretum. My son was just a newborn, but I'd felt guilty all summer that my enormously pregnant, crabby, hot and waddling self had been unable to frolic with my toddlers. So, inspired by the autumn sunshine and a suggestion from an October parenting magazine, we colored one paper bag red and one yellow for collecting (you guessed it) red and yellow leaves. So far, so good. In the back of my mind, I was probably hoping my then 3-year-old daughter, now with one week of preschool under her belt, would ask about photosynthesis.

Well, when we got there it was obvious that my tots wanted to bag the bags. The tree stumps were much more fun to climb, the leaves were more fun to crinkle and crunch, and sunshiny shadows needed to be hopped upon. We laughed and chased and tried to teach our 2-year-old "red light/green light" (she found the whole "red" thing a little limiting). We were covered with burrs and mud. We lasted maybe 45 minutes in the arboretum. We never made it to the Red Maple Forest, which was a little disappointing for a foliage lover like myself. But chalk it up as a connection. Just as much for what we didn't do as what we did instead—on our kids' own noisy, romping level.

64. NAME IT AND CLAIM IT

I continually hear parents complaining that their families never get to eat meals together. That they're always driving someone here or there. Or heading off to the gym. Or working overtime. Or the phone interrupts the one meal when they finally all do sit down.

Whose fault is this? Who overbooked the family, or allowed them to do so? Who answers the phone allowing others to interrupt sacred time? Who establishes the rules in your home? Who enforces them? Who rethinks them?

Ask yourself these hard questions. Figure out what your answers say about priorities. Decide if changes need to be made. If they do, make them. Or lay down some laws—perhaps make a rule that everyone comes to the breakfast table. Or limit one sport per season.

But stop whining about how you never have time to connect with your kids as though you have no control over your life. Reclaim it if you don't. Stop giving into adult peer pressure and the pace of the times that says, "The one with the most activities wins." It's a lie.

65. HAPPY BIRTHDAY TO YOU

BIRTHDAY

On your birthday (yes, *your* birthday), recount a specific and positive memory about *your* parents to your child. Perhaps it is the time Mom saved the spoon especially for you to lick after making cookies. Or when Dad gave you a piggieback ride. If you cannot seem to muster a happy memory, share with your child how sad that feels and let them know you desire to be a part of their warm and positive memories.

Then go on to talk about what the gift of your own life means to you. (If you can't celebrate the gift of life, what can you celebrate?) Hit some of the highlights, peaks, lows, and trials—but especially hit your victories.

Let them know in spoken and specific words that you are happy you were born.

66. Happy birthday to them

Birthday

On your child's birthday, recount the day they were born. Go through old photographs dating back to as close to their births as you can. (In today's world of technology, you can probably show them "moving pictures" of more than they'd even care to witness about their births! "Mom, what's that dark tunnel?" Mom: "Keep watching, daughter, because pretty soon you'll see the top of your head.") Paint them a word picture where actual photos are missing. (But probably not of the stuff in the previous parentheses.)

Be specific. Talk about changing those first diapers and what it was like to be sleep deprived. Recall how it felt when you nuzzled them close to your chest and witnessed their first smiles or roll-overs or steps or words. If you find your memory, for whatever reason, is short here, talk about more recent experiences with them that left your heart singing for joy.

If you find you cannot muster any heart-singing moments regarding this "assignment," commit yourself to making next year's gift to your child one of their best yet: that of a more joy-filled and complete parent.

67. MIX IT UP

BEING IN-LAWS

My swell friend Mary Gingell rocks at finding what's good in life, as shown by the way she embraces the expanding lives of her adult children. She is not only a mom but a three-time mother-in-law. Mary entered mother-in-lawing the same way she enters just about everything else: with enthusiasm and an inviting spirit. She loves new possibilities, is always on the lookout for them, and knows how to administrate them into reality.

Desiring to embrace her daughters-in-law, she not only included them in the Gingell traditions, but she began a new one the year her first son got married. Together, the two women made a giant batch of Chex Mix while the men watched a video. Of course the goal was not only to have snacks for the holidays, but to spend time together. To embrace the women not only as extensions of the family, but children *of* the family as well, transcending the stigmas sometimes attached to the word "in-law." Even before the next daughter-in-law was "official," she was invited into the "Gingell Women's Christmas Chex Mix Night."

68. HANDLES

Each new phase of our parenting (diapers, car pooling, dating, college, weddings, and so forth) brings a new set of challenges and opportunities. How we view the new situation will determine how we handle it. In other words, if we chose a handle of anxiety and sense of loss, that is what we will experience. If we make up our minds the new phase is simply the happy progression of life, we will be happy—although every moment probably won't deliver a gust of "yippie"! There will undoubtedly be more yippies than if we expected disaster. I have learned that we pretty much find what we look for.

69. Hair Braids

(Provided by Donna Turner)

> *More happens during soothing rituals than we might imagine.*

୬୭ଡ଼ୡ

When there was no time to put my hair in rags to curl it, Gram would braid it. However, that led to a tragedy: Mario, the big creep who sat in back of me in third grade, put my braid in the ink well. When I came home with a blue-black braid, my grandmother shook her head, took out the braid and soaked my hair in bleach. I felt like an outcast. Even Schnietzel, Gram's German Shepherd, would have nothing to do with me. He ran to me joyously, took one whiff, and slunk off to hide under the dining room bureau. Gram smiled patiently, patted me on the head as she lifted the hair from the bleach, and washed my hair in her kitchen sink. As she dried it with a towel, she told me not to put my braids in any more ink wells.

Except at bedtime, my grandmother's own braids were wound around her head. My braids, bright and gold, were thick and—I thought—too fat. Gram had a wooden brush with metal bristles. When I heard that brush pulling through her long strands, it gave me such a feeling of calm and peace. For when Gram brushed her hair, or mine, we often talked about tomorrow, or lunches. On special days, she would give me a nickel for an ice cream cone from the corner drug store.

These rituals of love put my life in place as her hands put my braids in place.

70. Take a breather

Establish a synchronized amongst-all-family-members hour in your home, once a week, when everyone does nothing. No errands, chores, work, or extracurricular activities. Just *be*. Together.

71. TRAVELING ART

I once heard about a brilliant idea for all those pieces of art your children create. After they've had their moment on the refrigerator, collect them in a manila envelope that your child decorates, and helps address to Grandma, Grandpa, or Aunt Peggy. Then, send them off! They are bound to entertain and delight others. They'll disappear from your space...just in the nick of time for their replacements (sigh).

72. SIDE-STEPPING

(Provided by Gundega Korsts)

One summer I drove down to Chicago to spend just a few hours with my son, whom I hadn't seen in several years. He was briefly in town for training sessions. We met at the Shedd Aquarium. I came with a friend, to share with her my delight in both my child and the wonderful water creatures. My grown child and I wandered, watched, and delighted in each other, but didn't really talk until we stopped for lunch, when I chattered with both my friend and my son.

It turns out I said very different things to her and to him, and he was eager to take in all these new visions of his mother. I hadn't thought of the difference at all, until I heard her reflect back to me.

There is so much to share with my grown child, things I want to share and things he would want to be included in. Who I am and was and want to be. Where he came from. What events shaped us all. What ideas shaped us. What mistakes we made, and how we recognized and repaired them, or didn't.

It is so easy to talk with my friends. Why is it so hard to open some discussions with my son? Not every question has to be answered. Some can just be sidestepped. Now, when I want it to be simple to raise difficult topics or to tell new stories that matter to me, I just make sure a friend is present too. The sparkle and conversation that leap so easily between me and my friend now as easily include my son. It's as simple as making a brunch date for three.

73. But wait, there's more!

When your child gives you a gift, don't just use or display it. Take the time—a week, a month, or many years later—to let them know how you enjoyed it (still do), used it (used it all up; it was so swell), looked at it (again and again), and remembered it and them in the process. They cannot know what you're thinking, so tell them.

74. Change the scenery

Throughout my growing up years my parents took us on picnics. Sometimes we ate homemade fried chicken and other times we picked up hot dogs, cold cuts, and bread on the way. Sometimes we drove quite a distance to a favorite respite and sometimes we only ventured to a park in town. Sometimes we took fishing worms and poles and sometimes we just took a blanket. But we always took us to be together.

Changing the scenery seems to open the opportunity for discussions. Perhaps it's because distractions—such as phones and televisions and piles of mail—are out of our site. But most importantly, we were in each other's.

75. Wanna-bes

Many, many years ago, there were quiet threads of rumors being sewn throughout our community that gangs were beginning to infiltrate the western suburbs. When authorities were queried in our area, they all but laughed, saying the only thing we had in our fine town were a few gang wanna-bes; the idea was considered absurd.

I wondered: Who do gangs recruit from if not those who "wanna be" in them?

A few years marched on and occasional squabbles broke out in the high schools that were rumored to be gang related. But no, they weren't *really* here, we were told, because outsiders were driving in to cause all that trouble; they weren't rooted in our addresses.

But I wondered: How do we know where gangs are rooted?

A few years marched on and dress codes disallowing hats in the schools were put into force. It seems gang members recognize one another by colors and things they do with their hats. Windows were occasionally smashed out of cars with baseball bats, a special gang law-enforcement task force was initiated to study things, a young man was beaten to death with a baseball bat—gang related and perpetuated by one of our area's home grown.

But I wondered: what takes us so long?

Get involved with your kids; don't give them a reason to think they need to belong to a gang to feel a sense of family. Read the papers. Educate yourself about things like gangs and drugs so that you recognize the signs, symbols, and actions. Sometimes things aren't in our backyards—they're in our homes. Be alert. Trust your kids but be alert...just in case.

76. Sing along

My son sent me an e-mail that made me laugh out loud. Although he talked about a few other things, he also mentioned he'd purchased some new music. He knew I would appreciate this news and what it meant because I, too, am a music lover and acquiring new tunes always psyches me up.

But what he went on to say, in the shortie line that captured my snickering grins, was, "I had to replace one of my CDs because skipping CDs are not good for singing along." Throughout the rest of the day I pictured him singing the beginning of a word over and over like a hiccuping goof. More grins.

Along with knowing he likes music, he also knows I know what he means by "singing along." We have done it together. Loud. Full volume. Harmony. Go ahead. Loosen up and give it a whirl.

77. SAYING GOOD-BYES

DEATH

(Provided by Kristine Johnson)
> *While we fret about life and the right thing to do, our*
> *children find a way to express it all.*

We've been to two already this spring. Last night, we drove to our third wake.

My toddler and preschooler ride expectantly in their car seats, the older one repeating what my husband and I tell him about our neighbor; how Mr. Rhodes became real sick and had to go to the hospital; how he stopped breathing at the hospital; how they won't be able to play ball with him anymore. Then we use the big D word—Mr. Rhodes is dead.

Do they realize that death is the opposite of life? How much of the subject do you share with children? As with life, there are more questions than answers. Of course, we don't know how much either one of the kids understands about the situation (especially when the 3-year-old wears his baseball glove into the chapel). However, we want to *show* them ("show" being the key word) in some way that death is a part of life. We don't want to leave them out of this experience.

Only a few family members remain in the silent chapel. My sons refuse to hug Mrs. Rhodes (I cringe), but as I rest the single red rose on the deceased's arm, my older son whispers, "Good-bye, Mr. Rhodes."

78. BATMAN LIVES

I opened the ringing doorbell to discover my 3-year-old son. He was wearing a towel pinned to his neck for a cape and an army helmet. His face was a muddy mess.

"Bret! Look at you!"

"I'm not Bret," he declared. "I'm Batman."

Now I open my ringing doorbell to find the face of my 35-year-old son when he comes home to visit. (That is, when he actually gets to ring the doorbell since I'm usually watching out the window and meet him at the end of the drive). I also recognize that same crooked grin when he deplanes.

Bret now snowboards on mountains, skateboards in arroyos (large cemented things that carry away running water from mountains), rides motorcycles, and does anything else that goes fast. Seems way back when, he knew he was born to fly and my job was to learn to soar in his backdraft. I still not only enjoy remembering his 3-year-old muddy story and sharing it with him, but claiming it when I study his man-child face and know that Batman still lives within.

79. Send a memo

My son was experiencing a stressful time at his job. I thought about how I could help, when I glanced upon an idea. There hanging on my office wall, encased in a plastic bag, was the small knot of spider-like, discolored remnants of his blankie. "Blankie," as the blue baby blanket came to be nicknamed, was what Brian used to clasp when he sucked his thumb. He would make a little puff out of one of the satiny corners and rub it under his nose while he slurped away. No matter how stressed or chaotic a moment might be, he could grab hold of Blankie, whip it up to his face, begin sniffing, and he immediately became calm. I wished I had a Blankie of my own.

Well I took Blankie from the wall and placed it on my scanner. I attached the picture to an e-mail with the header, "Just pretend you're taking a whiff," or something to that effect. Brian got a kick out of the gesture, but I also hope he received the hope that life would once again be okay.

What gesture or piece of the past can you think of that would serve a calming purpose or reminder for your child? Why not activate the best way to "send" it?

80. YOU RANG?

When I asked my friend Rhonda Kelloway if she had any pearls on how to connect with children, she didn't hesitate a moment to share a profound bit of connecting wisdom. "Yes, My mom came when I asked," she said. And for her, that said it all.

She was referring to a recent time when, as an adult in her own home, she found herself in need of her mom's experience and expertise. Rhonda and her husband Kirk had undertaken a major redecorating project and were working to a deadline to accommodate a large family gathering. She was up against the wall for time, knee-deep into a new experience, and much in need of a mother's advice and support.

"My mom came when I asked." Yes, that pretty much says it all for any of us.

81. MAY DAY!

MAY DAY

(Provided by Charleen Oligmueller)

Sometimes it just doesn't matter if everyone gets the point, as long as you do.

Two years ago, when my boys were two-and-a-half and one, we made May Day baskets out of paper plates and pretty ribbon. They decorated their baskets before I stapled them together and added ribbon. Then I put the baby in the stroller and the three of us walked around the neighborhood together on May Day, picking dandelions, lilacs, or whatever else we could find blooming and put them in our basket.

I'm sure they had no idea what we were doing or what May Day was all about, but it made me feel good that we were doing the special observance together, whether they "got it" or not.

82. Ahhhhhh...that's better

When I would watch my son grab his blankie and suck his thumb, then see the calm that washed over him, I longed for a blankie of my own. (I still do, sometimes.) But as we age, it's just not practical (or wise in the business world) to haul blankie or the much worn teddy bear into round-table meetings, lunch room duty, or the barber shop.

What "blankie-type" activity or physical thing do you turn to calm yourself down? Is it reading a good book? Deep breathing? Twiddling your thumbs? Praying? Chatting with a friend?

Talk to your child about your process and other *acceptable* adult methods to help you through difficult times. Then share some that are bad choices, such as alcohol or drug abuse. Present a few different scenarios wherein the moment of choice might be theirs.

83. Pajama Party

(Provided by Lori L. Gregor)

When my daughter was younger she loved to have Dad or I "spend the night." This meant a real pajama sleep-over in her room. We would sleep in sleeping bags on the floor, snack, and stay up late talking about "stuff." She did most of the talking. What a great opportunity to really get to know her.

Now that she is 15 and a sophomore in high school, we don't spend the night much but we are used to long tuck-ins and it is still a good time to talk about life's important "stuff."

84. The value of nothing

I received the following diatribe—a personally relatable diatribe—in an e-mail.

> *"Just the other day, after a friend mentioned the various lessons, activities, and camps her sons would attend this summer, I thought how it seems parents of today*

focus on being sure their children are accomplished *but not whether they are* happy. *Parents don't know if kids know how to just "be" or if they can value and appreciate any time that is not structured and goal oriented. I'm not against learning, but can't a kid just sign up for Little League Baseball without being sent to baseball camp beforehand to get an edge on the other players?"*

There is much to be said for striving for excellence and I certainly do not oppose one giving one's best effort. But my friend's questions are important. Very important. Worthy enough to spend a little down time pondering. Are *you* able to gear down to do that?

85. IF YOU BUILD IT

My dad raced harness horses for a hobby. When I was just entering 6th grade, we moved from our suburban home to a 16-acre hobby farm in a slightly more rural area. My folks did this not only because they were looking for more room for their children to roam, but Dad was happy to have a place for mares and foals and small bits of training. Mom welcomed ample room for bountiful gardens and multiple clotheslines.

One of our first projects on the farm was to turn the old downstairs portion of the barn from a dairy area to a place for horses. This meant we had to get rid of all the cement floors and cow stanchions and build stalls. Although we had help with the cement removal, we constructed a solid bank of stalls for various animals (mostly horses) from scratch. For weeks, side by side, my brother, Dad, and I measured, hammered, carried, and fit until at last our transformation was complete.

Build something of lasting value with your child, even if your only option is to use Lincoln Logs. There is something in creating together that bonds parent and child.

86. On the road again

When I was a divorced, single mom in my late 20s, there came a weekend when my mom and I decided to just take a road trip. Grandpa said he'd babysit so the gals said adios!

Where did we want to go? Away. What did we want to see? No dishes that we had to wash. What did we hope to do? Relax, eat, sleep, and maybe get our hair done. What time would we be home on Sunday? Whatever time it took us to return from wherever we'd finally arrived. We decided we'd just become modern day cowgirls and head out exploring, not even looking at a map. We'd eat when we got hungry and get a place to stay when we were tired—or beforehand if we decided to go to a show or something. We began our journey by picking a road and heading left.

We had a wonderful time, just the two of us. We ate, talked, drove, and explored. We'd get lost, find a town, and get our hair done. We discovered lots of cool places and things, but mostly we discovered more about each other.

No matter what the ages of yourself or your children, there are places to go—in the world and in the depths of each other. Unstructured time along with no destination is the best way to get there.

87. Treasure boxes

FATHER'S DAY

(Provided by Rhonda Reese)

> *We keep memorabilia because each piece is cloaked in a story. Here, in one tiny box, a human slice of a real man—foibles and all—who was honest and present for his child is captured. A daughter's heart lovingly beats in the midst of them.*

Before today dawned I sat with a treasure box in my lap and slowly poured through the priceless contents. It's not your typical treasure. In fact, if a burglar broke in he'd probably toss the items, and I'd be forever grateful.

You see, my special box is jammed with "dad stuff." Letters, a few pieces of his jewelry, a watch, poems along with other deep ponderings he put on paper, a tape recording of him reading a book to me, a collection of silly notes and such, all folded neatly and stored in a favorite flowered box. Each piece of my peculiar treasure brings a flood of fun memories and often, a few tears.

My father got promoted from Tennessee to Heaven one Tuesday almost three years ago and, wow, do I ever miss him. Not a day dusks that I don't look up at the clouds and wonder how and what Dad is doing on the other side. It makes me weep. It makes my smile. As another Tuesday nears, I'm grateful again to have had such a neat dad. His wit, his willingness to trudge through problems, his honesty about personal shortcomings, and his bravery displayed while working to overcome alcohol and anger problems, continues to challenge me.

One of my most telling treasures is a tiny jar filled with broken glass. Dad and I had a knock-down drag-out argument over that busted window. In the end though, we both won, collapsing into a puddle of laughter at the stupidity of fighting over such a dumb thing. At first light, I watched a violet striped sunrise and sent up a "Hi Dad, have a great day" prayer. Then I prayed that people around me would take time to hug their special dads and tell these still earthbound guys how much they're loved.

Treasure boxes are great. But treasured, tangible, touchable dads are so much greater.

88. STONES THAT SKIP

I cannot remember exactly where we were or how old I was, but I do know it was my dad who taught me not only that rocks can skip across water, but how to make them do so.

I do know it was the property on which I was raised that I learned how to pick wild raspberries along the creek. My "bestest" (sic) friend Eenie and I would meander along the bushes, sun beaming down on our youthful heads, plucking those delicacies, reddening our fingers and tongues, occasionally even putting one or two in the bowl. (Although we usually ended up eating those too, before we got home.)

I do know it was my cousins who taught me where to find crawdads in the creek that ran through their Indiana farm. And when the water got really deep at the bend, well we didn't catch crawdads there, we went swimming.

Expose your children to nature, even if the biggest patch you can find is a nearby park. Inspect. Discover. Be the one who presents the opportunity.

89. TIME FOR A CHANGE

The day we brought Brian home from the hospital, I was greeted by a blessed surprise: My husband offered to change his first diaper. Now, George wears a size 13 ring and was the younger of two siblings. Diaper changing wasn't something he'd ever practiced and Brian's entire body looked like a miniature doll in George's grasp. But sure enough, a diaper he changed and he went on to change them throughout all of Brian's diaper wearing years. It's a story I love to share with Brian as he then knows that from the day he came home, his father was hands-on willing to be involved in his life.

If you have a spouse, share precious moments you've observed between them and your child. Let them in on what they can't yet know or don't notice—especially since a little endearment can carry us such a long way!

90. SARRAH'S DOLL

(Provided by Phyllis Ludwig)

When my granddaughters turn 6 or start kindergarten, I buy them an American Girl doll of their choice. This year when our Sarrah turned six, I asked her if she'd like an American girl doll. "No, not really," she replied firmly. The more I thought about her answer the more I began to understand.

Sarrah developed Alopecia at the age of 3. This is a condition of the autoimmune system which causes all the body hair to fall out. At some point in our conversation, I thought to ask her if perhaps she'd like a girl doll without hair. Her eyes lit up and she replied with a resounding "Yes"!

I visited a local doll shop and explained my situation to the owner. She was willing to remove wigs from dolls until we found one whose head was acceptable, bald. (Not an easy find!) We dressed her in jeans and a baseball cap—just like Sarrah. The owner trimmed a wig into a short style but didn't glue it on. The new doll was ready to go and was she ever cute!

When Sarrah opened her birthday doll, she smiled and said she liked her. But, it was when I showed her how the wig could be removed that her beautiful blue eyes lit up and a big smile stretched across her face. She put the wig in the backpack (hasn't taken it out since), turned the baseball cap around backwards and was delighted with a doll that finally looked like her!

I learned how important it is to be affirmed for who we are.

91. Testing, testing

(Provided by Jennifer McHugh)

My mother used to have "taste tests" with us. She would blindfold us and put different items out and let us pick what we liked best. For instance, she would put three different name brands of peanut butter and let us pick, or put out Coke and Pepsi to see if we could tell the difference.

This was one of my favorite memories as a child and one that I have shared with my three children.

92. This for that

I'm not sure why it is kids become selfish, but there comes a day when everything is "mine"! Of course, this doesn't matter if it belongs to them or not. What they're holding is theirs and what you're playing with is theirs. What he's getting ready to pick up is his and what she looks at is hers. They just don't have enough arms to hold everything that is theirs. We do our best to extract these items from their hands and explain that they need to share. But sometimes all that ensues is fits of anguish or tantrums.

It occurs to me that sharing is kind of an odd concept to grasp when you have no framework to draw from. All they know is that you're trying to take something away from them. Perhaps a better way to transmit the message is to begin by teaching them how to trade through one-on-one exchanging.

Learning to share is a good lesson for lots of things in life.

93. HANG IN THERE

I remember my Grandma Landers hanging clothes on the line. She had long wooden clothespins with no springs in them. She kept them in a faded pocket made of cotton that she slid down the clothesline in front of her. Before each item was secured to the braided cotton line stretched tightly between two T-shaped poles, it was exuberantly snapped in the air. Each pair of coveralls or pillow cases made a loud popping noise before it took its place in the line dance.

I recall watching my mom hang clothes on the line one day. There was a storm quickly approaching. She scurried along the length of the row, unclipping clothespins as fast as she could go, tossing them in the clothespin bag she slid down the line in front of her, scooping the growing bundle of clothes into her arms while the sound of thunder moved ominously nearer.

As I inhale the fragrance of my own line-dried sheets, I picture my mom's face buried in the top of her bundle, and grandma's hands that smoothed and folded the laundry. I am one with these women of substance, fresh air, and task. I witness my son hanging clothes on the line and I am blessed yet again by this simple labor.

Share with your child a procedure you use that has been passed down. One day when you're gone, perhaps they'll feel the same kinship with the ages, their family, and a few things that blissfully stayed the same, such as rolling cookie dough, changing the car's oil, using duct tape, or "knitting one and pearling two."

94. Ask and you shall receive

We all cling to moments that mean something to us; we celebrate knowing when we've delivered one to another person. Ask your child what you've done that he or she liked especially. Then, ask yourself, have you done it again lately?

95. Cracking the code

Carol Burnett is famous for making America laugh. However, one of our favorite moments during her show was when she'd pull her ear, giving an inside signal to a family member. Our family had it's own signal: Throughout my developing years, whenever we were in a crowd, I knew when one of them was trying to get my attention when I heard the "family whistle." It consisted of a high pitch and then a lower one—sort of like how a coo coo clock would sound if it whistled. I'd hear the whistle and turn to the direction from whence it came. Sure enough, one of us would be standing there waving a hand in the air, acknowledging a roundup.

Does your family have a secret signal? If you do, discuss how it got started, if you can remember. If you don't, invent one.

96. Daughter's Day

Adoption

(Provided by Jacquie Cannon)
Connections happen when we're honoring the individuality and specialness of our children, and there are oh so many big and small ways to do that!

My mom had a special day that she set aside just for me. It was called "Daughter's Day." It was celebrated every year on May 15th, which was the day I officially entered her home, because I was adopted. It was like a second birthday, but it was so much cooler because it was a unique holiday just for us.

My mom died on November 5, 1998 and it was very difficult to face my first "Daughter's Day" without her. Before she passed on, she had been talking about how excited she was that this would be our 30th "anniversary" together. For her funeral, I wrote a tribute to her which included the description of this special day.

97. LET THE GAMES BEGIN

My friends Joyce Lohrenz and Donna Chavez are true believers in family. (And the more family members you can gather together, the merrier. And the more diverse the gatherers' age ranges, the better yet.) But what's the point of gathering together if you don't interact? And what better way to get people doing that than via games, each of my friends have concluded.

One of the games they both really love is an interactive mystery game. (The script for such a party can be purchased in any party store.) Each family member is assigned a character from the script. Sometimes Donna, a writer, writes her own dramas. Many family members might have fun taking a real family scenario and dramatizing it.

Each "character" (and aren't our families wrought with them?!) is given a set of clues they must dispense during the gala, along with regular mixing and visiting. The story usually goes along these lines: A crime has been committed and everyone needs to discover "whodunnit," giving all participants reason to talk to all participants rather than picking select corners and planting themselves.

No one is left out during socials like these. Our children are made as much a part of the festivities as the elders. And who knows, you might discover lots more about them by the end of the evening than simply figuring out who done it.

98. CAUGHT IN THE ACT

Let your child "catch you" reading one of their favorite books when it wasn't their idea. Not only might you be surprisingly entertained (I usually get more out of the children's sermon in church than the one for the adults!) but it'll give you something specific to talk about.

Allow them to lead a mini book club discussion. Set up another club meeting, letting them choose the favorite book this time. Post a notice on your refrigerator—perhaps even hang a photocopy of the book cover—and invite the entire family and a few neighborhood friends: big and little ones; parents and kids—all enjoying the favorite stories of a child.

99. ONCE UPON A TIME

HONESTY

A young friend of mine would tell me stories about things that were happening in his life. Some, of course, I knew weren't true—but rather wild exaggerations mixed with doses of fantasies. Although I admired his storytelling ability, I didn't like that he tried to pass them off as truth. I wanted to keep the friendship in tact, and yet do my part to help him stop telling lies (which was in effect what he was doing).

However, it occurred to me one day that I would not be serving one of his superior gifts if I convinced him to stop using his fertile imagination. I would, in fact, miss the stories and perhaps keep the world from one day meeting this great author or playwright. The task became more one of separating story from reality and helping him to know when each was appropriate.

The next time we met and he started in with one of his tales, I applauded his ability to tell me such a *wonderful* story. I also told him how much I valued our friendship and wouldn't want mistrust to get in the way. I drove home the fact by telling him how it was a brilliant story even if it wasn't the truth. In this spirit, I asked him if it *was* the truth or a story? He thought a second then said somewhat sheepishly, "Story." I told him again what a great storyteller he was and then thanked him for being such a good, honest friend. Now, several years later, his stories continue to amaze me and his truth in other matters means all the more.

100. UNBORED GAMES

(Provided by Kimberly and Justin Warner)

> *Spend an evening observing how your family spends an evening; then ask yourself: Is this the way it should be?*

I'm a single parent of a 9-year-old boy. Justin's a sweet kid, into your standard kid things: Pokémon, Star Wars, Playstation, etc. He is very video oriented.

However, I realized one night as he sat watching a movie and I sat in the next room at the computer, that we sat apart way too much. So this past Christmas I asked my sister to get Justin the Star Wars version of the Monopoly game. I had already completed my shopping for him—all Pokémon!

We both have enjoyed that gift—it surprises me how much we do! When we sit down to play, I am always Qui-Gon. Justin varies his "men," but he usually chooses Jar Jar Binks. We play—sometimes for hours, sometimes just for a short time—laughing at our good or bad luck, getting in and out of jail, building towers and hoarding properties, reciting lines from *The Phantom Menace* as we go.

It may be a new twist on an old board game, but more importantly it is a new link between me and my son!

101. BEATING HEARTS

While sitting in the airport, I witnessed one of the best reunions I have ever seen. A woman and a boy deplaned and were greeted by another woman who stood grinning, waiting expectantly. The two women hugged one another and exchanged a brief, friendly word. Then the greeter kneeled down, swooped the little boy into her arms and exclaimed, "I'm so excited to see you that my heart is beating *so* fast." She then put the child's hand to her heart, pressing it close so he could feel it pounding away.

Words are great, but somehow it becomes all the more believable with the actions to back them up.

102. Don't answer

While watching television this morning, I heard that a legislator was trying to pass a bill to keep telephone solicitors from calling between 5 and 7 p.m. in order to keep them from interrupting dinner with our families.

I was thinking, "*Just don't answer the phone!*" Why do we need a law? Why do we allow every ring to interrupt us during the only time during the day we break bread with our children?

I remember reading a book by the Delaney sisters who lived to be over 100. Finally, only in their later years and upon the insistence of caring relatives, they put a telephone in their home. A short time afterwards, they had it yanked out, seeing it as nothing more than a chance for others to violate their peace and quiet and interrupt their meals. I don't think we need to go *that* far, but we do have a choice about when we'll let it rule us.

Perhaps we should say, "This time together with you is more important than anything anyone has to say," when we hear a ringing phone.

103. Me too

ILLNESS

Over the years my adult men-children have occasionally phoned to say, in their most pathetic voices, "*Moooom*, I'm sick." (Neither are married as of this writing; this will one day be their wives'...um... pleasurable experience.)

"Oh, that's terrible! I wish I was there to make you tea and honey or buy you some blue Popsicles," I lament. Tea and blue Popsicles always have held magical healing powers in my family, beginning back in my childhood when my mother introduced me to them.

Although my mom has been gone for decades and it's been nearly 40 years since her hand applied Vicks Vap-O-rub to my chest, I can still feel her healing powers simply by smelling the jar. Oh ye great parental physicians, heal thy children with more than drugs.

104. GO FLY A KITE

INTENTIONAL DISCONNECT

I was visiting Tom Wilburn, an old family friend who lives on a plantation in Mississippi. While there, he told me a most amazing and refreshing story. He recalled a lean time when he thought he might lose the plantation, which had been in his family for decades. The heritage of this land hung on a mere loan application.

In the midst of this gut-wrenching stress, it came over him that the thing to do was to back out a bit. Inhale. Make a kite and go fly it. And so he did. And wouldn't you know the loan officers appeared on the spot to peruse the land and interview him, right after he'd launched his creation. The men in charge of his land's fate showed up while he was flying a kite! Amazingly, he received that loan. He told me that following his instinct to fly a kite is what, in large part, procured it.

Taking a break from the worry and having some fun to release his stress—two things which always refuel us—produced clarity of thought. The bank guys trusted the wisdom of a man who knew what he needed and went after it. They told him so; him flying a kite and telling them why is what saved the plantation during a very dark hour.

I grew up with this model of perspective on things. When a business decision or problem would envelop my father's attention, the next thing we knew, he'd be golfing or fishing. This is a man who would work 24 hours to get a job done in time. But he was wise enough to know—and teach—the difference between the need for "nose to the grindstone" and a "dose of perspective" that could only be obtained by backing off. Answers came, he said and proved, during the breaks.

Dig deep, if need be, to find this wisdom. Teach this to your children. Model this to your children. And perhaps that can be done best by stopping what you're doing to go fly a kite with them.

105. THE HEART OF THE MATTER

(Provided by Paul Halvey)

> *Listen to the questions. No matter how old, listen to the questions. They just might be ones for which you need an answer!*

Sometimes a toddler can ask a question that truly cuts to the heart of the matter. Bridget and I were both napping when she woke up and called out, waking me—thankfully—from a dream that was a senseless jumble of images. In the dream, I was struggling to read and write some computer code, but events and the code were caught in a loop and nothing was working or making sense.

Over some post-nap juice, I asked how she slept. "Fine," she said. I made a reference to my looping dream. Then she asked the question that would have set everything straight not only in the dream, in the waking world as well: "What were you trying to do?"

106. PRESENT THE OPPORTUNITY

When Cecilia Wall's husband and his father bought a 1932 Ford, they unintentionally found a way to stay connected. Together, they spent relentless time converting it into a stock car for racing. Although they never drove the car themselves—they solicited others more experienced in that arena—a lot more was accomplished than simple car conversion and maintenance. They really got to know one another and shared trials, tribulations, victories, and ongoing lessons about sportsmanship.

As Cecilia and her husband had children, they, too, got involved—three generations with heads under the hood.

"It wasn't an easy thing to do," Cecilia said, "because it was so expensive, but it surely was a great opportunity. The whole family used to spend time together at the races every Sunday."

107. STOP THE WORLD

"Daddy, will you play trucks with me?"

"I'm making breakfast now, honey. Maybe after I eat and before I leave for work."

"Mom, will you make me a peanut butter sandwich for lunch?"

"I've got to get the clothes off the line before it rains. The peanut butter is in the cabinet and the bread is in the 'fridge."

"Dad, you can't believe what happened today."

"Can you tell me about it after I check my e-mail, son?"

"Mom, can Megan stay over tonight?"

"Not tonight! I've got a briefcase full of reports to go over, Susan!"

❖ ❖ ❖

Most of these exchanges happen without any eye contact. *Stop!* Will you one day be looking at the back of their heads as they wave over their shoulders when they're saying goodbye? Moving out? Moving on?

108. IN CONTROL

"Before you can control an animal, you better have control of yourself," said sage family friend Tom Wilburn. Tom has been around many different animals throughout his life. We'd been swapping stories about obedience training for dogs, corralling sheep, and training horses. I immediately knew I was hearing truth and that it applied to child rearing.

Sometimes...sometimes it seems to us that our children's lives are out of control. Why are they acting that way? How can I get them to change? How will I handle it if they don't? Will they ever, *ever* grow up? How many times can I ground that child? Wait until I get my hands on them!

Stop! Ask yourself: Am I in control of *me*? Do I need to get better at letting go? When will I begin to understand that they have a right to their own mistakes and lessons? What am I showing my children on how I handle tense situations? You'd better have control of yourself.

109. CHILD OF MINE

Brian once sent me an e-mail explaining a difficult decision he had to make. While I was reading it, I was heartened on how mature and responsible he sounded. I was sittin' proud in my office chair. Then I came to his salutation, "Your little Bri." I actually gasped and put my hand to my heart at the words. They were a term of endearment I used when he was a youngster, and occasionally still did during special moments or when I was feeling silly. However, he never referred to himself as that. To see him claim it now, when he was in control of much, helped me feel his need to simply "be"—at least for one stress-filled moment—someone's child.

May each of us as parents never forget that we, too, are someone's child. And may we strive to represent a safe place for our children to simply "be" our children, no matter how many candles there are on their birthday cakes.

110. WHISTLE WHILE YOU WHATEVER

I was standing in line at an airport gate waiting to check in and the gentleman behind me was humming. I grinned as I related to this habit. "Do you know you're humming?" my husband often asks me when we're out in public. Or, "You're singing out loud," he says, as though I had no idea my mouth is open and sounds are coming out of it.

"Yes I know," I always calmly answer. "And I hope I never stop."

You see, my dad hummed and whistled, as does my oldest son. My mom hummed and sang, and my youngest son sings—and plays a mean air guitar. My parents' melodies were signs to me that joy dwelled within them and it just couldn't help but reveal itself out loud. They were gifts to me that enabled me to know, without a shadow of doubt, that even when things were bad, music calms the soul.

Now I know many people can be perfectly happy within without humming or singing out loud. But children watch and listen for signs. Why not whistle them a few?

111. REMEMBER WHEN

I cannot even begin to imagine how many times I heard my father tell the story about the time I was about 3 years old and we were eating in one of my folks' favorite casual restaurants.

"You wouldn't sit and eat. You were talking to everyone around, just entertaining them and yourself. Then, when it was time for us to leave, you started screaming and saying you didn't get to eat. You were throwing such a fit as we packed you up that people were giving us dirty looks, thinking we were starving this poor little girl who didn't even have time to chew her food."

Although the story would change a bit in detail, it was without question *our* story. My dad would no doubt think about telling this story when he would sit across the table from his daughter who still talks so much she is always the last one done dining.

Why not share one of your child's stories today? One that reminds her or him you've been paying attention for a long time, and are continuing to do so today.

112. CASHING IN YOUR CHIPS

I watched intently and with overflowing eyes as comedian Mike Myers shared with Barbara Walters his continuing grief over the loss of his father. He explained how life was like being in Vegas and that he'd won all these chips. The loss of his father, he said, equaled having the joy of all those chips but no place to cash them. Such was his relationship with his dad.

Yes, winning is something. But what good is winning when you can't share the news with someone who's known you the longest?

Are you a welcome and ready cashier?

113. SPEAK YOUR OBVIOUS

My oldest son Bret was recently home for a five-day visit that culminated with a baptism. This blessed occasion of his friend's first child, now Bret's goddaughter, was the reason for his return.

Usually when the boys come home, they do lots of running to catch up with old friends, which is the way it should be. The door revolves; they come and go. But this trip, Bret said he didn't tell anyone he was coming home but the parents of his goddaughter. He said, "I just want to visit with you guys, Mom." Although the actions of that statement blessed me on their own, it was *hearing* his desire that helped me receive and celebrate this precious gift.

Whether your child is 4 or 44, it is pure gift to say, "I enjoy spending time with you." And this I learned from one of my own.

114. BE A GOOD RECEIVER

Sometimes we can get so caught up in the duties and challenges of parenting that we forget our small children also have much to give and teach: instant forgiveness, welcoming hugs, delight in discovery, simple pleasures...the list is endless.

Stop. Look. Listen. *Receive.* The tomorrows, days of sagging dandelions, grungy little paws, body-slamming hugs, and warm wiggly bodies on your lap will soon be long gone. What will be left of those precious days is hopefully tucked away in the portfolio of your memory and it can only get there by being received in the first place.

115. MARKS ON THE WALL

MEMORIAL DAY

In a communication mix-up during a kitchen redecorating project, my husband, unbeknownst to me until it was too late, washed all the marks off our kitchen wall. Each of these dated marks let each of us—husband, wife, two sons, Wonder Dog Butch, and a few friends—know how much we'd grown (or shrunk, in my case) over the past two decades. On the verge of hysteria at the discovery, I wanted to scream but all I could do was cry. I ran to my office, slammed the door, hurled myself down at my desk, and sobbed into my hands.

All those spots where torsos were stretched, hopes of growth were held, stories were told, and pieces of lives were lived—erased. I remembered the face of each child checking for progress against their previous lines, against dad's height. I grieved that none of this can be recovered.

And then it struck me: It was Memorial Day and I was crying over marks on a wall! My memory of visiting the traveling Vietnam Memorial ("The Wall") flooded me. I was pierced by the memories of the palpable grief and irretrievable emptiness that cloaked that symbol of lives lived...and lost. Onto my knees I sank in prayer for parents whose children were never coming back again.

Then I realized, it is marks in the heart that remain, forever and no matter what. Perspective sometimes arrives cloaked in the depths of life laid bare.

116. THE MORE, THE MERRIER

On more than one occasion I've heard a parent wonder aloud how they could ever find room in their hearts for a second child. Taking it a step farther, they worry how their first child will be able to accept the addition as well.

Joan Wester Anderson writes brilliant stories about angels and miracles. But she also has a sparkling way to help siblings understand that more children isn't less love, but rather a multiplication of love. Although the ceremony described below was meant to help alleviate a sibling's concerns, I'm sure it would help adults who harbor the same worries about broadening *their* love with a newcomer. It is a procedure I've seen used at weddings, but this takes it a step further.

Gather together with candles. Light one to represent God's light, then the parents each light their candles from it. The sibling then lights his or her candle from the parent's light, along with another candle for the child who's just arrived or is on the way. Each new flame representative of the spread of love. More light, more love. More people to help you when you're down and cheer you when you're up. There is more of everything.

117. BE SPECIFIC

(Provided by Carolyn Armistead)

"How was school?", we ask the children every day, somehow unable to help ourselves.

And every day, the inevitable answer comes: "Fine."

Lately, I've begun to mix things up, throw them off balance, by asking more creative, off-beat questions.

"Did anything weird happen in science today?"

"Tell me something that made you laugh."

"Did anything make you say 'ew!' today?"

"Did anything make you say 'cool!' today?"

"Tell me one good thing and one bad thing that happened at school."

"What kind of mood was your teacher in?"

"What did your best friend have for lunch?"

Sometimes, before we know it, we're actually having a conversation.

118. I'M HAVING A BAD DAY

It was Christmas vacation and the plane was mobbed. Parents were traveling with their entourage, their accessories and necessities, and things were tight. I imagine there wasn't a passenger who wasn't wilted from the exhausting, jam-cramming boarding procedure. A father and daughter were finally seating themselves directly in front of us in the airplane. After wandering to two other places, getting the rest of the family and all their "stuff" settled,

Dad looked like he'd just lost his best friend. He plopped down with a giant sigh and threw his head against the headrest.

"What's a'matter Daddy?" his young daughter asked.

"Daddy's having a bad day, honey," he replied, somewhat dejectedly. "He's made a lot of mistakes today." What a tender hug and kiss Dad received, just for admitting his foibles.

What brilliant honesty. What integrity. What a good way to let his daughter know that she, too, can have bad days and admit them and that life will still go on. They will know that they will still be loved.

119. TRADITION!

(Hear musical background sounds from *Fiddler on the Roof*.)

One of my happiest moments as a parent came when our adult son phoned long distance before a recent trip. George and I were flying to Albuquerque. We were all meeting at our oldest son's for Christmas.

"Don't forget to bring the stockings!" he chirped.

My heart sang at the rewards of tradition playing out in the next generation. There is connectedness in the familiar and comfort in the rhythms of expectations.

120. WHAT'S IMPORTANT

"What do you want for Christmas, Mom?" one of my adult sons asked. After a bit of consideration, I sent him an e-mail: "I'd like a box of old-fashioned kitchen matches."

"Are you planning on setting a fire?" he queried back with what I'm sure was a smile on his face. Although I wasn't exactly sure, I did know why I suddenly wanted kitchen matches and I jotted him off my knee-jerk response.

"I plan on resurrecting the sheer delight of memory and method by striking one of those sturdy, powerful, no-fail matches. They bring me back to the past, prove their worth in practicality, and light whatever candle or incense is in my hand at the moment. There is magic in simple pleasures such as these."

Before I'd drawn a breath, I was sending another e-mail. "I've changed my mind. I don't want a big box of old-fashioned kitchen matches. I want several boxes of them. I want to spread boxes of those delightful matches around my house in order that I might have the security that they are there for the striking. Mom XO, who realizes that she has just, off the cuff and in reply to a simple question, written perhaps one of the most profound things she's ever birthed. I'm glad it's going to my baby, who I hope understands the truth of this correspondence and gets himself a few boxes while he's at it."

Talk about the simple pleasures, for your child's benefit as well as your own.

121. GOING AWAY GIFTS

(Provided by Phyllis Ludwig)

Day camp or college, thoughtful daily reminders of our love speak volumes.

When our daughter, Amy, was ready to leave for her first year at college, I knew it would be wrenching for both of us. To make it easier for both of us, I decided, because she always loved presents, that I would give her a dozen little gifts, one to be opened each day for her first two weeks away from home.

I spent the summer shopping for just the right items that would convey my love and encouragement for her. I bought things like blueberry soap from our trip to Michigan, apple butter from Wisconsin, and her favorite votive candles. Each one was wrapped in bright paper with a short poem or special Bible verse written on the tag and marked for the day it was to be opened. All the presents were placed in a basket and kept hidden.

When it was time for us to leave her at her dorm and let her get on with this new phase of her life, I left the basket on her bed to be discovered later. Each day as she opened her treasures she knew how much we loved her and supported this new stage of growing into a fine young women. (I cried all the way home, of course!)

122. SING ME A SONG

I recently sat across from a woman holding her new baby. Not more than a couple weeks old, the mother sat staring at her son. Studying. Taking in every degree of curve in his cherubic face.

While I embraced the site, the mother (and I) listened to an audio tape of the silky voice of a singer who had written a song especially for this tiny human. Her words and the sweet melody were a testimony to the love in which he was conceived and the assurance of God's hand in his life. For the rest of his days, that song will remain a testimony to this moment of wonder and the importance of his entry into the world.

Wouldn't it be wonderful if we each had our own song or poem or paragraph written, just for us? One that can be read or listened to when we're needing a boost? Whether it's your words and melody, your words sung to a familiar melody, or the talent of someone else who brings those words to life for you, why not capture the depths of your thoughts about the child you love in a format they might one day find themselves singing.

123. I LOVE YOU

Say it. Say it with words.
Say it with actions. Say it.
Say it again.
And again.

124. WORDS OF AFFIRMATION

Speak them.

125. GUESSING GAME

Using your finger, draw letters on your child's back and have them guess what letter or word you're writing. Your child will receive a welcome touch and a back scratch, while working on the alphabet. Have them do the same to you. *Ahhhhhh.*

126. ISSUES OF FAITH

I usually just delete mass forwarded e-mails without reading them. Reading each would take up too much time and I find real life much more interesting than regurgitated e-mail. Recently, however, one caught my eye. (How could I not see it; I received it 10 times!) This particular e-diatribe dealt with what the forwarders deemed were unjust boundaries on the public expression of a particular faith.

Whether I thought the justice of the facts were right or wrong, which had to be culled from the midst of searing and rather nasty shots at everyone—from the government to "freaks"— isn't my point here. My point is that this ranting, which was much more mean spirited than the offenses they were talking about, was zinging through the Internet in an attempt to stand up for God. Perhaps worst of all, the e-mail ended by saying that passing it on was a "simple test" of faith. The correspondence sadly struck me as a counterproductive bad attitude in total opposition to what I believe to be the tender, loving core of this faith, which is mine as well. As one who believes herself to be a child of God, it hurt my heart.

Whatever your religious persuasion, seriously consider how you represent God and issues of faith to your children. Are your views the ones you want your children to perpetuate?

I believe that pointing a child toward a faith-filled life is one of the most intimate, helpful, and important gifts a parent can impart. Children and faith are sacred; speak of them with reverence and gentle hearts. Positive connections are not made through mean-spirited rants. Historically and globally, those who did left a wake of destruction in their paths.

127. PASS IT ON

I do a fair bit of traveling for my job, which gives me many opportunities to speak with strangers. This morning's limousine ride was no exception—in fact, it inspired me. The gentlemen who shared my ride and I got to talking about the dregs of business travel. So many people think it's glamorous. In fact, it's exhausting and taxing. Business travel is the price we pay for getting to the place in order to do what we love (not to mention to pay the bills).

One of the more unusual topics we touched upon during our 20-minute journey was that of thank you gifts. I shared how sometimes I'm presented with a large basket of items in breakable containers. This, of course, poses a problem: How do I get it home when I've already packed my suitcases tightly for the outbound flight? My travel partner talked about a similar dilemma when he gets receives bottles of wine; he often juggles, packs them, or has to just leave behind.

But then he shared, with a quiet and reverent voice, the best thank you gift he said he ever received from a thoughtful client. It was a complete hot dinner, ordered, prepaid, and delivered to the home of his family, whom he was kept away from on the first nice weekend of the season.

Whether it's your own kids or someone else's, remember them. Honor them and honor those who long for their presence.

128. The laugh game

The laugh game is very simple. The first person in line lies on the floor, face up. The next person lies on the floor perpendicular to person number one, with the back of person number two's head resting on stomach of person number one. This pattern continues until the "family tree" is built.

Then person number one says "ha." Person number two then says "ha ha," and so forth. Before you know it, everyone is lost in fits of laughter. It'll definately be one for your memory portfolio.

129. The code

(Provided by Michael Lewis)

Develop special hugs that only you and your child share. We have a few: "Hugarino," "bear hug," "g'morning hug".... Each one is different and for different occasions.

130. LISTEN

No more. No less.

131, TOMORROW, TOMORROW

Do you feel lately like you often hear yourself saying, "I'll have to get to that tomorrow!" Just make sure your child hasn't become a "that."

132. I DON'T KNOW

Admit it when you don't know, then offer to find out. Ask your child if they'd like to help you.

133. THE NONCUSTODIAL PARENT

BLENDED FAMILIES

My friend Larry Humbracht is a multiple-time grandfather. Although he and his children's mother divorced years ago and he has not always lived in close proximity to his kids, his relationship with them today is a solid one. Today, both he and his wife (remarried) thoroughly enjoy the ties that bind them, one to the other around the circle of their families.

When I asked him what pearls of advice he'd have to give to a noncustodial parent, he said, "Stay with it. The kids might be a little put out with you for awhile (after the divorce), but they'll come around. Mine did. Just stay in contact, even if it's only a phone call every week."

134. SAY WHAT?

While collecting stories for this book, I encountered a mom who seemed particularly interested in helping me. "You must be captured by this idea," I said. "Perhaps you have some of your own stories you'd like to share?"

"Well," she said with a frustrated—albeit disappointed—tone in her voice, "I asked my son to share some of our bonding moments and he said we'd never had any." I couldn't help but break out in laughter! Ah, junior high school kids; gender doesn't matter!

When I shared this story with a dear friend who has two boys now out of high school, she, too, immediately laughed. She said that her sons recently asked her what they were going to be having for Easter dinner. She answered that they were going to be having what they'd always had for their traditional Easter dinner—the Easter menu they'd had every year of their lives. Neither of her children seemed to be aware that there *was* a traditional dinner. Again, I was guffawing. (Actually, we both were.)

The thing to take away from this story is that *all* parents can relate, in one way or another, to these disappointing moments. Tuck this piece of info away in your memory bank for the next time you feel disconnected from your child. Then, rest in the knowledge that you are universally connected in astonished and confounded ways with *every* parent and child in the world.

135. Keeper of the Words

(Provided by Jan Langford)

Juggling kids, job, housework, dance and gymnastics classes, Brownies, church, and volunteer work leaves little time to create charming photo albums commemorating family milestones. I feel fortunate to have somehow found time to photographically commemorate the *birth* of my children; yet undeveloped film cylinders from my 7-year-old's first Christmas roll in limbo at the bottom of my purse.

Although years behind with my photo albums, I take time to commemorate another aspect of my children's lives that can't be chronicled in home videos or pictures. When each child was born, I began a journal of their words. Baby babble, toddlers first words, and funny (and embarrassing) moments are chronologically assembled. I somehow find time to keep them current. We have spent hours cuddled on the couch, on long car trips, and in waiting rooms reading and rereading, laughing almost to the point of tears at the adorable sayings and pearls of wisdom of their childhood. Photos show what they look like, but their words show how they think and feel. I know that maintaining and reading these cherished books will always provide a wonderful way to connect with my children, and will give them a way to connect with their past.

136. PANCAKE ART

I was sitting in my dentist's chair, mouth agape, stuffed with cotton and other wads of stuff, and the dentist and I were sharing—to the best of my ability—tidbits about the past Mother's Day weekend. Knowing he was the father of two young sons, I inquired as to whether or not his wife had received breakfast in bed. So, in stuffed-mouth language, the universal language of dentists, I asked, "Gig oo ha ah ni moer a? I r ife ha rkst n e?" (*Translation:* Did you have a nice Mother's Day? Did your wife have breakfast in bed?")

"No. She'd had a girlfriend sleep over night the night before and they rolled out pretty late. They did, however, have breakfast waiting for them in the kitchen," he replied. Turns out he had made pancakes, one of his favorite leisurely morning rituals when he doesn't have to go into the office. It just seemed fitting for Mother's Day. He shared that his sons loved it when he makes pancakes.

"Oo oo ake r oys icky ouse ancake apes?" (*Translation:* "Do you make your boys Mickey Mouse pancake shapes?")

"Oh sure," he said. "And I also make butt-shaped pancakes. (I hear him laugh out loud at his own statement. I nearly choke on my cotton wads.) I have boys, you know, and they just think those little butts are the funniest thing to ask for." He then giggled again, as though he was a child himself. And so did I. (And thankfully I didn't choke to death.) And so, I imagine his future grandchildren will one day create traditional family butt-shaped pancakes.

Do you have anything as fun and fascinating as butt-shaped pancakes in your family? Why not?

137. HUFF-²-N-PUFF

Recently I was busy making my 50-year-old brother a birthday card using a program on the computer. On the face of the card, I placed a photo of a little boy wearing a dorky, pointy, cardboard birthday hat held on by elastic under his chin. He is leaning over his birthday cake which is aglow with candles. He is captured in this photo—as every family member is every year on our birthdays—with his cheeks extended like a puffer fish in mid-blow, expelled breath not fully yet reaching the bending flames.

Although I had to mail this card many states away and I would not be with him to share this year's birthday moment, I knew when he was reading the card that we would be sharing a connection with not only one another, but our deceased parents as well. A connection established throughout all the years of tradition honoring and celebrating the gift of our lives.

Thanks Mom and Dad, for finding so many ways to connect your children together.

138. KIDDIELAND!

For as far back as I can remember, my parents used to take me and my brother to an amusement park about 15 miles from our home. We loved that place, not only because it was fun, but our parents were also a lot of fun when they took us there. My folks often told the story about how charged our anticipation would be. They both claimed that Jimmy and I could be fast asleep in the back seat on a trip *not* scheduled to go to Kiddieland. But if we got within a mile of the place, we would both suddenly pop up awake and scream, "*Kiddieland! Kiddieland! Kiddieland! We wanna go to Kiddieland!*"

One recent Mother's Day morning, I awoke with my usual mix of emotions: happy to be a mother; missing my own mom, decades after her death. The boys weren't going to be home for the holidays (they usually don't; we save up for other events) but I knew I'd be hearing from both of them. George and I had no plans, so he asked me what I felt like doing.

"I'd like to go to church, then I want to go to Kiddieland and ride the train," I said. "I'd feel close to my mom there." He's used to me by now, so he said, "Fine." And so we went.

We stood in line and when George started to buy two tickets I screamed, "No! Just get one! You have to stay here and wave at me when I go by!" Because he loves me—and again, after 30 years he's used to me—that's exactly what he did.

Of course I wept nearly half the ride, but they were tears of gratefulness for parents who would make it a point to have fun with us. They neither ever looked bored or duty bound but rather happy to be a part of the fun, waving at us as we circled around them through life.

139. Fly baby, fly

INTENTIONAL DISCONNECT

When my first marriage fell apart after four years, my 3-year-old son and my 22-year-old self (yes, you read that right) moved in with my parents. It was an intensely painful time; one I wouldn't wish on anyone. Gently, carefully, and without judgment, my parents enveloped us in their shelter.

After a few weeks, my father invited me to the kitchen table, a familiar setting. First he reviewed my life up until that moment: I had lived at home, bound by house rules until I went to college; I stayed in a dorm—bound by college rules until I impulsively got married after only seven months of classes; had an unscheduled child 11 months into the marriage which ended school and bound me to family life. He assured me I had been loved by he and Mom through each stage. This I already knew.

Then, in a statement that took great courage and selfless love, he delivered my walking papers and what would ultimately be one of my most grateful, defining moments in life:

"You need to know you can make it on your own as a woman and mother," he said. "You need to find an apartment." Although I was a bit stunned and somewhat afraid, I trusted my father's trust in me. I learned that I could depend on it.

The two years Bret and I lived in our tiny, rather sad apartment, were difficult times. I struggled through work and daycare and never had enough money. But they taught me perseverance and how to make wise decisions, sometimes learned through the consequences of my bad ones. They taught me how to let go of what didn't matter and to value what did. My parents' self control to let me struggle through on my own rather than rescue me or pad the comfort level was an honoring connection with my personhood for which I will always thank God and them.

They cheered me on; they grounded me; they set me free to fly.

140. JUST DON'T SAY NO

Oprah had a show on one day highlighting children who had done amazing things. They had raised incredible amounts of money for those in need; they had given sandwiches to the hungry and delivered teddy bears to kids in hospitals week after week.

One of the things I noticed was what their parents *didn't* say. They obviously didn't say, "You're too young to do that." "Where'd you get that crazy idea?" "Who do you think's gonna help you pull that off?"

141. HELPING HANDS

(Provided by Christa Tanner)

Last summer my daughters, Casey, age 9, and Jamie, age 7, planted flowers for their 95-year-old great-grandmother. She was so thrilled that she never stopped talking about how much this act of kindness meant to her. Inspired by her response, this summer the girls will began enlisting the support of 40 of their friends for the "Kids Dig Up Northbrook" project. They will each be responsible for identifying three elderly folks in their neighborhood who are not able to plant their own gardens in front of their homes.

On a Saturday in early June, these kids, along with the help of some adult drivers, will plant flowers in their yards, thanks to the donation of annuals from a local sponsor. I have been helping the girls write all the correspondence, as well as assisting them with the organization and sponsor solicitation. We are enjoying the chance to work together on something which makes a difference in the lives of others.

It's also a great lesson for my children (who have everything life has to offer) that giving is much more rewarding than receiving...such a great life lesson for a mother to reinforce early in her children's lives.

142. Ultimate connection

Whether your child is one minute or 60 years old, there are times when you are simply not connected, be it physically or emotionally. Perhaps they're in the other room; perhaps they're in another country. Maybe they're an honor roll student; maybe they've lost their way in life. You might be feeling inadequate in your parental abilities or feeling temporary shutdown; they might be running from your grip or rebelling against your authority.

No matter what, there is always a way to be powerfully connected with them for the greater good of everyone...and that is through prayer. I truly believe that as long as you are praying for a child, they are never lost from you. In prayer, you are unbound by human limitations. Prayer changes, heals, relinquishes. Prayer is a first line of defense and offense and a stopgap to hopelessness. Prayer is a parent's ultimate connection which can never be unplugged.

When you don't know what to pray, try this, "*God, thank you for loving my child, no matter what. Amen.*"

143. Ah yes, I remember it well

I asked Bret, our 35-year-old son, how parents could stay connected with their kids. Without hesitating a moment he answered, "Stay young yourself."

"What do you mean by that?" I asked.

He explained that parents would do well to remember their own youths. Rather than calling them silly or rambling some diatribe about youth today, they might recall the passion of their own "youthful" choices in music and entertainment. Rather than just whining about so many of the things kids do today, he said, maybe they could try joining them first before making a judgment. Or at the very least, they simply shouldn't make condescending comments around every corner.

If you feel somewhat convicted by this, be encouraged that it's never too late to change course. It's never too late to begin "zipping a lip" rather than firing disapproving slips of the tongue. It's not too late to apologize for snap and harsh judgments about something you're not really acquainted with. It's never too late to remember your own youth and cut some slack to those who are in it.

144. AVOID AVOIDING

There is nothing you can do to guarantee your child won't do drugs, aside from keeping them locked in a cell all their lives. Of course I don't encourage this choice. (Most days.)

I do believe the best way to insure against them making a wrong choice concerning drugs—or anything else that's dangerous—is to stay connected, insuring them that you care. You need to listen. You need to respond. You need to pay close attention. You need to admit your mistakes. You need to talk about times when decisions have been difficult for you.

But what if they do make a bad choice and get drunk at a party? What if they do get pregnant or shoplift a pack of cigarettes? Will they have been seasoned to confess, having been nurtured and grown by your previous forgiveness (along with appropriate consequences)? Will *they* understand that *you* understand, because you've made bad decisions too? Will they feel free to come to you in a time of trial, knowing mercy, good counsel, and unconditional love reign in your home? Have you assured them it does? Do you act like it?

Have you been fair in the past with discipline, making sure the punishment is no more severe than the crime? Have you worked at testing whether the "crime" is truly a serious one or is it just a ding to your pride and ego (bad parent, rather than misbehaving child)?

If a child gets in trouble, the last thing they want to find out is that you're more concerned with how it might affect you and your reputation as a parent rather than them. And they learn how you respond through the little things.

145. MEMORY MAKING

TRAVEL

(Provided by Phyllis Ludwig)

As a parent and now a grandparent, I have always considered myself to be in the "memory making" business. My own mother modeled this for me with my children as she is a great storyteller. Whenever she was around, the kids would always ask her to tell the events of their growing up experiences. They never seemed to tire of hearing their own stories. She also had trips or special events she did with them as various rights of passage.

One of the rights of passage I do with my grandchildren is "first trips." Train rides at age 3, plane rides at age 5, camping trips, and so forth. On these excursions we take pictures that we later put in albums along with stories of the things we did or saw. As they get older, the children illustrate these story events with their own pictures and writing. These albums are favorite reading material when they visit our house. They also have become chronicles of not only the experiences we shared but the heritage of family, the preservation of their childhood—and equally important—the conversation and laughter that we share during these very special times. Memory is as much for me as it is for them.

146. LINE GUARD

(Provided by Carrie Elsass)

A great way to become closer to my "tween" son and get him to open up is to play what he enjoys right alongside him. He loves basketball. While I'm quite untalented in that department and don't particularly enjoy the game, his respect for me for making the attempt to connect with him (and attempt to play basketball) is obvious. He longs to talk with me about teams and players, and I find myself woefully inadequate (and unfortunately uninterested). I imagine that as he cruises into his teenage years I will become quite the expert so that we can continue to connect and converse frequently.

My 11-year-old still regularly asks me to read a book he has devoured and enjoyed, or to listen to and sing along with his favorite song of the moment. Answering these requests comes much easier for me than a slam dunk so I am all too happy to oblige.

I worry sometimes that suddenly lines of communication will magically disappear when he becomes a teenager, but in my heart I know that it couldn't occur in a day, so I must be ever-vigilant to make sure such a day never comes!

147. ACCEPT THE VILLAGE

(Provided by Martha Rohlfing)

> *Whether it's news of your child's birth through the heart of another or encouragement on a day when Mom and Dad just seem to be pathetically ill-equipped, one of our children's greatest resources is the care, enthusiasm, and guidance of others who care about them...and us. May we be smart enough to welcome and encourage these people.*

I have never been married and I have no children, but I thoroughly enjoy my role as an aunt and great-aunt. (In fact, one of my goals is to be a great great-aunt, and, someday maybe a great great-great-aunt!) I believe the extended family, such as aunts and uncles and on down the line, can often reach children in ways that parents cannot.

One of my favorite ways of connecting with the children in our family is to tell (and retell) them about the day they were born—what the weather was like that day, when and how I heard the good news, what I was doing when the call came through, and, most importantly, how happy I and everyone else in the family was that this wonderful being came into our family.

148. WANT WHAT YOU HAVE

(Provided by Tom Wood)

> *A wonderful lesson on how to frame the family picture .*

Mom and Dad raised seven children in a four-bedroom house which only had one bathroom. When her friends told her they

were amazed at how we could manage in such limited living space,
Mom would always smile and explain how much she thanked God
that we were a close family at least. Otherwise, it might have been
a problem!

My dad's post office job was sufficient in providing for our
family's needs but very little remained for any luxuries that many
of my buddies enjoyed. Even our first television set was a used
one, and Dad needed a part-time job to fit it into the budget.
Oftentimes we needed to take turns holding on to the antennae
just to get reception on that old Admiral TV set. If we complained,
Mom would just look around and ask where Dad was that night.
She didn't have to say anything more because we knew he was at
his part-time job.

Each summer I would listen to the plans that a friend had for
some exotic vacation where he would travel to on an airplane. At
our supper table I would talk about those plans and ask Mom where
we might go on vacation. Her face would light up with pride telling all of us seated around the table how happy she was when
Dad's application for a week's vacation in July had been approved.
She wasn't sure just where we could afford to go, but at least we
would all be there together. Somehow, that sufficed to make each
one of us smile.

In our family we did not have everything that we wanted. Mom
just made sure that we wanted everything that we had.

149. Doin' nothin' time

Breathe in. Breathe out.

Breathe in. Breathe out. Breathe.

Do not try to learn something today. Do not try to be a more
perfect parent or get better at anything. Just breathe in. Breathe out.

From the diaphragm: Breathe in. Breathe out. Breathe.

In your respite of refreshment comes an openness and a re-
charging which allows you to more fully reconnect with your kids,
and yourself.

150. PERCEPTIONS

I love New Orleans! It has everything: food, sauces, jazz, food, the river, ships, ethnic diversity, food, the French Market with food markets within, the French Quarter, a delightful trolley, history, the blues, museums, food, an aquarium, and more.

I heard someone telling about dreading their upcoming trip to New Orleans. All that dirt and unsavory stuff. Smells bad in the summer, they said.

Your children usually believe what you tell them. There are two sides to every story—*every* story—and often they're both true. Make sure they get both of them.

151. DON'T PANIC

I recall sitting on a porch with neighbors who, as of that moment, obviously didn't have kids yet. A little boy came dawdling down the side of the road, feet keeping their own perfect rhythm—you know what I mean—when he came upon an empty garbage can left in his path by the garbage man. Without missing a stride or beat he kicked it over and kept walking. He didn't kick it maliciously or with any intent to damage it.

"Why in the world did he do that?" the man next door asked.

Me, mother of two sons—who recently tried to change the channels on my TV with the cell phone rather than the remote control—knew full well. Stuff happens. Kids just do things sometimes. (Parents just do things sometimes as well.)

"Because he kicked the garbage can," I said matter-of-factly. "It was there in his path and he kicked it." There was no more to it than that. This was not a child who didn't turn out to be a juvenile delinquent, a petty thief, a high school drop-out, or a neighborhood vandal. (I happened to know him and no it wasn't one of my sons—this time.) He was just a child who kicked a can in his path.

Remember this story the next time you find yourself screaming, "*Why? Why would you do such a dumb thing?!*" at your child and they answer, "I don't know." Don't let your mind run rampant with fears of *this* undoubtedly being the first step toward his or her slippery slide to demise. Remember your last doofy mistake or impulse. Look at yourself in the mirror, noticing that *you* are not in prison. (And if you notice that you *are* in prison, know that your child is *not* you.) We all do dumb things. They are not all thought out or on purpose—we just did them.

152. SHUSH!

(Provided by Kim Rimay)

Don't say a word. Just hold them in the quiet and let them know they are loved. This works for any age—adults too!

153. YULE TIDINGS-US-OVER

(Provided by Jan Kwasigroh)

We had a daughter. Then 11 months later, we had twin sons. So when they each left for college, our empty nest came quite close together as well. I decided prior to Thanksgiving of the first "fledgling flight" to do something special to tide us over till our daughter, Kim, returned for the Christmas holidays. It was so popular that it became a tradition with each of our children that lasted throughout their college years.

I found an 18-inch artificial tree and got a teeny string of lights and a dozen or so teeny ornaments. I figured out how many days between her return to campus after Thanksgiving and her return home for Christmas. I then bought and wrapped a small nonsensical gift for each of those days, for Kim and for each of her roommates. (I couldn't leave them out! Some years I had to get 23 teeny gifts for each one!) I'm not talking huge gifts, but just something to keep the season present (and keep us in their thoughts). I'd send things like a package of fake fingernails, plastic rings, small rolls of vitamin C drops, teeny decks of cards—anything for a laugh and fun. I'd send the tree, along with instructions stating that each child had a gift for each day and that they could only open one day's worth at a time.

The tales that I heard made it easier not being together during this pre-Christmas time. I heard stories about how the girls played "dress up" and did their nails while studying for finals. My sons reminisce about the card games they and their roommates made up at 2 a.m. Sometimes I'd fear I'd picked something "really dumb" — such as the vitamin C lozenges, but then I found out later that all the girls had sore throats at that time and they were really needed. It was truly a "God" thing!

The trees were returned when they came home at Christmas and we all looked forward to the next year's experience.

154. Organizational duty

Being one who loves organization but who is usually never fully organized, I cannot relate to parents who have a place for everything and everything in its place or are driven by distraction to clutter. (I always need just one more organizational implement from the organizing store!) Personally, clutter is sometimes my friend. I travel a lot and it seems the first thing I do when arriving in a hotel or motel room is to clutter it up a bit with my good and sacred stuff. Make my nest familiar, so to speak. I'll bring a certain candle, a few glow-in-the-dark stars, my Bible, reading materials, clothes slung here and there, miscellaneous colored pencils, snacks (always snacks), and other stuff. (If you have a child like this, know that I've turned out to be a pretty responsible and considerably joyful adult!)

Nevertheless, I'm always open to change. I even went so far as to once buy a book on the topic of organizing. (Of course I haven't found it since I bought it. It's no doubt at the bottom of one of my piles.) I listen to organizational and "declutter experts" when they're on TV. In fact, recently one of them said something that rang my chimes: "Organizing isn't getting rid of junk but identifying what is important." There are lots of layers to this thought—including those that apply to parenthood—that have nothing to do with physical organization. Let's *all* think about that. (Hear that, Charlene?)

155. Out of the mouths...

Years ago my sons and I met up with a friend and her young daughter. When I said hi to her child, the blond beauty grabbed hold of her mother's leg and buried her face into mom's slacks.

"She's shy," my friend stated about her daughter, "aren't you honey?" Mom reached down and stroked the head of her daughter. When she heard this about herself, she all but entirely disappeared behind her mother. If the child had any doubt about how or who she was, it was just affirmed. How could she do anything other than live up to it were she to please her mom?

Perhaps she wasn't shy. Perhaps she was just hesitant and simply needed to hear that I was mommy's friend and Brian's mother. But now, she was shy. She had heard it. What do you tell your children?

"You klutz!"

"Why do you always spill things?"

"Are you ever going to amount to something?"

"You are bad."

Be careful before you speak. Your child my actually be listening and believing what you speak, whether it was the truth before that or not.

156. Fear not

FEAR

Oh my, what do we do about this statement to reassure our children? I once read where childhood is the place we learn to deal with fear—and no doubt that's true. So what did we learn about fear when we were little? How do we, the parents, deal with it now? Do we act as if it isn't true? Face it head on? Run from it? Does our behavior reflect how we'd like our children to handle fear? Do we need a bit of retraining on the topic?

There are books written on this topic so I'm surely not going to pretend to be giving the ultimate answers here in 200 words or less, especially since I am not a psychiatrist or a psychologist. I am, however, going to toss the following statements out for your consideration. They may be able to help you connect with your child's fears:

    ▨   "Andrew, I believe you are afraid. But here's a great thing to learn about being afraid: You don't have to stay that way or let it stop you from moving ahead."

▩ "Shelley, I know you're afraid but together we'll face it."

▩ "Gregg, fear can be a good thing since it sometimes keeps us from making mistakes. But it can also be a bad thing when we allow the feeling of fear to overrule what we know must be done."

▩ Jason, I remember when I used to be afraid of darkness and now I can't go to sleep when the light's on."

▩ Kimberly, the best way for us to face fear is to look it in the face."

My mother had a plaque hanging on her wall. It now hangs on my kitchen wall where I can be reminded of its truth: "Fear knocked at the door. Faith opened it. Lo, there was no one there."

157. BRINGING HOME THE BEST...AND THE WORST

(Provided by Jodi Brandon)

When I was growing up, my family had dinner together every night and we went around the table, each sharing the high and low point of our day. At first my siblings and I weren't into it, but then we found that it was really a great way to find out what was going on in everyone else's lives. Why they were down, why they were so happy, etc.

Now my fiancé and I engage in this enlightening activity at our own dinner table every night. It's a tradition I hope to pass on to my own children.

158. ROUND TABLE

The child of one of our friends was getting married and our entire family was invited, including our teenage son. Seated together around a large round table, the "oldsters" who had been friends since childhood (aside from a few spouses) inevitably began to swap stories and reminisce about their wild and crazy youth. It was not often this old gang had a chance to be together in a leisurely fashion; the race was on to cover all the favorite, most endearing, outrageous, and horrific memories.

As the evening wore on, the stories became more detailed, more hilarious—or hysterical, depending upon how you looked at it. They also became and more revealing, especially to our son who was not missing a word. In fact, he looked as if he was joyfully filing away what might one day no doubt be regurgitated as timely evidence or ammunition! Uncensored stories that we might not otherwise have shared with him (for obvious reasons) were enthusiastically being spilled by the "grateful-for-the-memories" gang and lapped up by the "delighted-for-the-knowledge" youth.

All in all, I'd say it was an inspired opportunity for truth and reality. If you truly desire to be connected (perhaps even more than you think is humanly necessary), make sure such opportunities exist.

159. Remember whose you are

(Provided by Jan Limiero)

The teenage years must have been both joyous and heartbreaking for the father of four girls. As our interests turned from Daddy to boys, friends, jobs, and futures, Dad must have been both proud and terrified to watch his girls grow up. But he never let on. He stayed as calm and collected as always. But he also did one thing that has lasted a lifetime: Dad never let one of his girls leave the house without a simple reminder. (Or was it a threat?) Whether we were leaving to go to work, on a date, or off to college, he would look at us with a smile both tender and stern and say "Remember whose you are!" That one phrase reminded me of my identity.

What teenager isn't seeking his or her identity? I didn't have to seek far because my dad reminded me almost daily. I was part of a family, a heritage. I was part of a bigger whole. I belonged. But, I wasn't just Merton Dibble's daughter; I was a child of God. What a sense of security to remember whose I am, even to this day as a mother of three.

160. Open door

I hardly ever recall my mom saying no to a request for friends to eat or sleep over, whether they were mine, my brother's, my dad's, or hers. The door was open to everyone at any time. She didn't fret if the house wasn't in perfect order or we weren't having something special for dinner. We shared what we had and the way things were.

She taught me the gift of welcoming and modeled that people always mattered more than appearances. Always.

161. ACCENTUATE THE POSITIVE

I recently had one of those days when the tyranny of the urgent pulled me this way and that. I was grumbling about something to nearly everyone I came in contact with who casually said, "How are you?" I'm sure they were sorry they asked since I happily (gross misrepresentation of attitude) emptied both barrels of my frustrations—even to complete strangers.

One of my tasks involved filling and sending 37 mail orders after a speaking engagement for which I'd run short of books. Since I never expected to run out, I'd casually announced I'd send them free of shipping charges should I run short. Little did I know...And so I grumbled my way up to the window, two giant baskets in tow, having spent an entire day labeling and packaging, "happily" telling the window clerk about my tactical, expensive mistake.

"Why not consider this a random act of kindness," she said. Babing! Yes! Why not! Brilliant! I often recommend this type of thinking but in my own life, it had completely alluded me! The moment I turned my heart and attitude, I also realized these orders were a gift of bounty to me! Duh! Yes, this was a random act of kindness on my part.

Next time you're in "martyr mode" and it involves your children, think of your actions as random acts of kindness. "Yes, this is a deliberate act of random kindness that I'm choosing to cook dinner tonight." "It is a random act of kindness to repeat the instructions for the 70 billionth time." "I am applying one more bandage to an owie I can't even see as an act of kindness." Speak it out loud within their earshot. What a wonderful thing to model. What a great way to connect without grumbling. What a difference an attitude adjustment can make!

162. Fribble me this

(Provided by Chris Hendrickson)

I have found the best way to connect with my kids is over a shake that we like to call a "fribble." (A Fribble, coincidentally, is also a shake that Friendly's makes, although ours is completely different.) You simply add ice cream, milk, chocolate, or whatever you want to add with the first two ingredients, blend it together in a blender, pour into a glass and then sit with your child and just talk. Ask about school, ask about friends, ask about anything you want. Ice cream does wonderful things when it comes to getting your child to open up!

It also helps to look them in the eyes while you are drinking your fribble. Even a teenager gets a wide-eyed look of pure enjoyment and love for their "fribble maker" as that ice cream goes down!

163. Look see

A friend of mine e-mailed me photos of his beautiful daughters. I responded by e-mailing him how beautiful his young munchkins are, harkening back to days when my sons were wearing Halloween costumes and diapers. I added the following note.

"On those bad, tormenting, tired, frustrated parenting days, just visit your own photos. There are pieces of your heart running around out there."

Your mission for today, should you choose to accept it, is to study those perfect and darling photos, especially if this is a day when your kids are anything but that!

164. In their time

(Provided by Donna Turner)

> *Timing is everything. Like the old Kenny Rogers song—*
> *which certainly applies to more than card games—know*
> *when to hold 'em, fold 'em, walk away, run...or patiently*
> *and with wisdom and honor, wait it out.*

Our son Scott had a hard time learning to read. We thought we could correct the problem by reading to him, and having him read to us. The fact that he did well in school encouraged us and we assumed everything was okay. When he was in high school, however, his history teacher called to say that Scott was failing his class. He said, "You know, he does well on everything I cover in class, but on all written material, he fails." Every time we tried to broach the subject to Scott, he denied any problem. "The teacher doesn't like me." or "I just wasn't paying attention." We offered help. His response was, "No way!" I had enough sense to painfully bide my time knowing that he had to want help for it to be effective.

One night he came home in the middle of a big party and said, "Mom, I need to talk to you." I went to the bedroom, closed the door and the first thing he said to me was "I am not stupid." "Of course not!" I replied, "We never once thought you were." "Well, then," he asked, "why can't I read?"

Although we didn't know it at the time, Scott had dyslexia, a neurological problem which makes it hard to perceive and record words without distortion. He saw words one way in his mind and wrote them down another.

With professional help, his reading speed tripled in three months. I won't say he's a prolific reader, but he is a university graduate and a playwright whose plays are produced from coast to coast. All his plays show a kindness for others who struggle in many ways, a product of his own struggles. As parents we didn't do everything right, but we tried to listen, respect, and honor our children as their own persons. For Scott the connection was made in his time, not ours.

165. MORE THAN IT APPEARS

Occasionally, our oldest son used to bring home test papers on which he'd scored very poorly. One of the things I'd notice, however, is that when he didn't know an answer, he entertained himself (not sure if he entertained his teachers or not!) by filling in humorous, wacky answers that were actually sometimes hysterically funny. Of course I'd try not to grin since I was wearing my "Dark Dangerous Disappointed" face.

Today he is a very responsible adult who continues to have a sparkling sense of humor. He is blessed with long-standing friends, the gift of storytelling, and the ability to laugh at himself. I tell you this as a sign of hope so on days when you are wearing *your* "Dark Dangerous Disappointed" face you can continue to look for all the possibilities in your child's future.

166. TELL ME A STORY

(Provided by Will Kilkeary)

My daughter and I often interrelate on our long car trips by storytelling. We invented a basic story. It began with a green and yellow butterfly that looks like it has the letters "G" and "B" on its wings. (We are from Wisconsin which instantly makes us Green Bay Packers fans.) As we try to get closer to the butterfly, it leads us into a nearby woods where a magical opening appears in the hillside. When we follow the butterfly into the opening we find that we are in fairy land and that King Oberon and Queen Titania have a problem which defies their magic but which they hope human ingenuity can solve. Here the storytellers take off on their own.

We take turns telling these stories and can vary the start to fit the story. My daughter often has the butterfly fly around our cat or dog until we take them along, and then uses them in the solution to whatever problem she has created. It chews up miles, it is a delightful way for us to get comfortable talking to each other about varied subjects, and I often see where my daughter uses these stories as a vehicle to discuss real-life problems that are bothering her; they too bring us pleasantly closer.

167. ROLE REVERSAL

FEAR

My friend Mike really likes not only the movie, but the message of Disney's animated movie, *Beauty and the Beast*. He looked forward to watching it with his 4-year-old daughter. She, however, was afraid. The beast was just too scary.

Then Mike hit upon a way to not only help ease her fear but to engage her in the story. He pretended he was afraid of the beast and asked his daughter to help him move through his fear. With the role of protector suddenly bestowed upon her, he watched the tides turn as she talked him through the elements. How the beast wasn't real. How it was just a movie. How he was nice in reality, but just looked scary.

Mike gave her a cause to help conquer one of her own beasts, that of her own fear. Way to go Dad!

168. WHAT WE LEAVE BEHIND

(Provided by Janine Glinn)

My mother had recently passed away and I was hungry for anything that she had written to me, so I dug out old letters and reread them often. As the youngest of nine children, the memories that my mother shared of my first words, and so forth, were often a conglomeration of my brothers' and sisters' firsts. I only had two pictures taken before I entered kindergarten. I realized that when I pass away, I wanted my son to have something to hold on to that would tell him how much he means to me.

I started a scrapbook when he was about 2 years old. The book covers his life from day one through today, at age 4, and we often page through it together, laughing at the silly things he has done and the sweet moments of our lives together. He says, "Wow, I don't remember doing that" to just about everything more than a year ago. I know that this gift that I continue to make for him, and also for his baby brother, will become even more precious as the years go by and as I include cute things they have said and done.

I know that my sons will never have to wonder from where they came. They will each know how much they were loved, in thought, actions, and captured memories.

169. EN GUARDE!

Perhaps I've been too influenced by Zorro movies over my lifetime, but I've always been attached to the saying, "En guarde!" I can almost hear the chink of metal against metal as the sword is swiftly wielded from its shield. All systems alert! Be ye prepared! Eyes open! Aiming right at ya, Bub!

Wouldn't it be wonderful if we, that quickly and with as much focus, wielded our complete attention toward the presence of our child? (Feel the sudden roll of eyes zooming left; see the cavernous ears hurling open; watch the smile spread across your sincerely interested face...and then across your child's.)

170. What if...

A friend of mine came home from a time-management seminar and said the facilitator asked two provocative questions. The first was, "What is the one thing you could do to improve your relationship with the person you care the most about? (For the sake of this illustration, let's say it is your child.) Each attendee didn't have to think very long before writing down their answer. The instructor waited until he saw no more penning action, then he just stood there in silence for a spell.

And then he asked the second question: "Why haven't you already done it?"

If that isn't a gut punch to the child-rearing stomach, I don't know what is.

171. Oldies but goodies

My Grandpa Landers was a delicious character. He loved to laugh, loved to tell stories, and loved me. I was privileged to be around him a few times a year when I was growing up, even though my grandparents lived several hours a way.

I always relished when Mom, Aunt Del, and Grandma went out and left Grandpa babysitting me, my brother, and my cousin. Not only did he brag on our behavior when they returned, but he usually spoke the truth because we had such a good time with him, we were not inclined to dream up trouble on our own.

Something I learned about Grandpa during those spells was that he loved music. His favorite song was "Dark Town Strutter's

Ball," an oldie-but-goodie classic. The song was enthusiastic and upbeat, just like Grandpa. My mom requested it whenever she could, long after Grandpa was gone...and until the day she died. I always knew why. I request it when the opportunity arises.

There is comfort in singing the song my mother's father used to sing. It is a melodious reminder of all those who loved me. It is also a reminder that children often live up to their expectations: Expect the good.

172. DO SOMETHING

It doesn't do any good to just sit and fret about drugs, alcohol, gangs, and all types of other evils your children might encounter. Solid, involved, present, and connected parenting on the home front is an active solution that is much more productive than tying your guts into a knot, losing sleep, and turning into a screaming lunatic. No, this won't help prevent negative alternatives and might in fact drive your kids to them. So begin with staying connected.

But there are more steps you can take to be involved on an even broader scope. They'll not only show your kids you are serious about caring about their youth (a connection beyond your personal connection), but your broader associations will undoubtedly lead you to more parenting resources. Get involved at your child's school or church. If you see your community is putting together a council on youth, be there. Pick any youth advocacy group and join in.

A simple place to begin looking for ways to reach beyond is right at your computer. The Partnership for Family Involvement in Education organization might inspire you and their Web site has tons of sources. Check it out: *pfie.gov.*

Many folks are out there caring about our kids. Join them.

173. TECHNOLOGY KNOCKS

I love accessories. Love them. And some of my favorites are steeped in personal connection with my kids, such as the mug I had made for each of us with a family photo on it. I also rotate new photos my kids send me electronically as I use them for the wallpaper on my computer. I'm currently booting up every morning to a picture of Brian and Jake, my new golden retriever "grandpuppy." He's (Jake, of course) standing up on his hind legs, leaning his front paws on Brian's shoulder (he's squatted way down) licking Bri's cheek. I can almost smell the divine puppy breath. The delight in my son's scrunched up face as he receives these kisses of love is of course why he sent it to me. He just knew I'd say "Ohhhhhhhh!"

I've seen mouse pads with mug shots; screen savers with family quotes scrolling across them; posters; cardboard, stand-up cutout photos that look like paper dolls, and more. Technology is becoming limitless in its abilities to allow us to look and see those we love, even in the midst of our piles of work.

Give ye thanks and participate!

174. THE LITTLE ENGINE THAT CONNECTED

When our children were young, one year we decided to take a train from Chicago to Albuquerque, N. Mex., to visit my parents. Rather than drive or fly, because we've done both, we geared up for a leisurely, scenic adventure. The Happy Baumbich Family would travel on the train. Due to expenses involved, we did not get a sleeper or private car. We camped out in a main car, "sleeping" in our seats which reclined (sort of).

Here's what I remember: Chasing Bret through the train; waking up at every stop because I'm a light sleeper; wrestling someone on my lap; eating expensive food in a sometimes rocky setting; and thinking to myself on many occasions, "Are we almost there?"

Here's what else I remember: Our entire family's excitement at looking forward to the adventure; sunsets that took our breath away; ample time to talk and study each other's faces (we were seated two-by-two facing one another); my own childlike thrill that matched that of my children's as we passed through dark tunnels; and being very happy to get there and share our great train adventure with grandma and grandpa.

Here's what my kids recall. Brian: "I don't even remember the trip." (He was very young.) Bret: "Not much at all. I do, however, remember taking a trip home from Albuquerque by myself once on the train."

"Oh, what do you remember about that?" I asked.

"Being on the train for a long time." (This is my *active* one, remember.)

What is the lesson in all this? *I* remember. I remember the good, bad, and dubious adventures with my children because we took the time to take them. And boy do I have the stories to tell, whether anyone else remembers them or not!

175. A TRIP OF ONE'S OWN

FEAR

Bret recently reminded me of a train trip he took. He traveled home from Albuquerque, N. Mex., by himself where he'd been visiting Grandma and Grandpa. (No, this isn't deja vu; you just read about it in the last section.) His recollection sparked my memory of a round-trip train ride I took alone when I was in high school. My parents let me travel from Illinois to California on the California Zephyr to visit my cousin.

I remember many details from the train ride out there because it was during the holidays and the train was filled with military people on leave. All those handsome guys to chat with...and chat I did. I also remember details from the train ride home (which I'd been looking forward to for obvious reasons) but was disappointed because it was *not* filled with military people (read: *guys*) or any other interesting people. Instead, I was seated next to a lady who complained about teenagers for two straight days.

The reason I like knowing my son and I both took solo trips is because they are filled with that connectedness of trust between parent and child. Not that there weren't natural concerns about allowing a child to travel alone (yes, I remember this, too) but because parental concerns did not interfere with the natural progression of life. Our kids grow up and we need to realize that.

176. WHAT'S THAT?

It's a matter of personal taste: I happen to be one of those people who don't "get" Picasso. I happen to find sparkly rocks and most refrigerator art much more beautiful than anything I've seen of his. And yet, he's obviously valuable to the world as a great artist; that I respect. (And he's certainly valuable to those who have paid tons-o-bucks to collect his work!)

I also don't happen to recognize the name of many other renowned artists. Nor am I educated enough to recognize periods or styles (although I might actually take a class one day), but it doesn't stop me from enjoying them. Studying them. Wallowing in the color and creativity and diversity and having my humble (yet loud) opinions.

Maybe you're like me; maybe you're not. Maybe you're shaking your head at my uncultured self. Perhaps you're muttering, "Well if I was that ignorant, I certainly wouldn't tell everybody!" What matters isn't what you think of me. What matters is that you be bold enough in *your* personal ignorant soft spot to admit it. (I've heard some people have never heard of a White Castle Hamburger!) If it's fine art, don't let it keep you from exposing your children to high culture, such as art museums, opera, and theatre. Your children are *not* you. They might "get" what you don't. It might become one of their passions and they'll have you to thank for it.

177. ROUND AND ROUND WE GO

Growing up, I recall me and my brother, Jim, driving go-carts, racing my dad around a track at one of those rental places. I also recently ran across pictures of my brother driving the make-shift go-cart dad helped Jim build (I was busy with boys by that time) for him to drive around on the farm.

No, you're not too old to drive a go-cart, swing on a swing, or slide down a slide. So what if you creep along, don't pump too high, land on your butt in the dirt? It'll give your kids something to laugh about! Dignity be darned and your kids will love it. And right now, I dare you!

178. SOUVENIRS

TRAVEL

A friend of mine recently announced, with a look of exasperation and defeat on her face, that her son wanted to go to the Wisconsin

Dells for summer vacation. Now, Wisconsin is green, lush, and lake filled, rich in natural resources that astound, delight, and refresh. For those of you who have never been to the Wisconsin Dells, picture this: Many fenced-in deer which you can feed by putting money in a vending machine for pellets, pretty scenery nearly totally camouflaged by souvenir stores and tourist traps, loads of places to eat junk food, water ski shows you pay to see, expensive rides in boats that can go from land to water, body-to-body tourists....Ahhhh, every youth's vacation dreamland.

I laughed and acknowledged my friend's reluctance. However, at the same time, I applauded their upcoming excursion because I very well remember *my* family's trips to the Dells—from both sides of the parental fence. In fact, I took a moment to give thanks for the dumb souvenirs my parents let me buy (within a reasonable and established budget) that reminded me of our journeys together. I give thanks for the memories surrounding my children's dumb souvenirs at which I, too, raised my eyebrows. Things like leather coin purses with beads stitched on them that seemed like "real Indian stuff" but were probably "made in Taiwan." Cheap toys that touted "Wisconsin Dells." Moccasins (of course, there were moccasins). I give thanks for all those small reminders.

If your children should ask for a vacation piece of junk, just remember that to them, one day that piece of junk will remind them of their family vacations—and that's worth lots more than plastic!

179. FAMILY TREASURES

My grandmother phoned me long distance one afternoon. She was crying. My mother, her daughter, had, within the last year, died suddenly at age 56. Grandma, like myself, was still raw with the freshness of death.

"I need you to come down here right away and get this mirror," she said, then she wept some more.

"What mirror is that, Grandma?" I asked.

"The mirror I have hanging in the living room. The big one with the gold filigree trim and the wide bevel."

"Why do I need to come get it?"

"Because your mother used to say, 'Mom, one day when you're gone, the only thing I really want to make sure I have is this mirror, it has so many memories for me.'" And now, defying the typical laws of order, Mom was gone before *her* mother and grandma was left with the one thing Mom wanted to remember grandma by. Because I was the closest familiar link, it should be mine, grandma declared, and she needed me to come get it right away so she could have the comfort of knowing it had been passed along.

Is there something you have now that your child would like the joy of receiving from you while you're still here? Pass it on.

180. What do you do for a living?

Some time ago, "Take Our Daughters to Work Day" was invented. Being the mother of two boys, I wondered what goofy person thought that prejudiced holiday up and didn't they realize boys were special, too?

Of course I was a full-time homemaker so it was moot to bring them to "work." They'd both already seen my work every day of their tiny lives, up close and personal. Frankly, they were probably as sick of it as I was on many of "those days." It seemed counterproductive to tour our home to show them what I did. Dragging them from washing machine, to toilet bowl, to underwear drawers, to the vacuum sweeper and back, while wagging my finger and pushing flyaway strands of hair out of my face seemed to be a negative experience. (Can you even *imagine* the horror of being my child on one of "those days"?)

My dad, however, had taken me to his workplace dozens of times over my growing years, way before someone had to invent a holiday to get people to do it. I guess the holiday, even if it is gender neutralized, makes sense if you need a holiday to remind you that your kids are curious about you. Don't feel like you need to be reminded, okay?

181. A shelf of one's own

I used to belong to Kiwanis, a service group that strives to make a difference in people's lives around the globe. One of our projects on a local level was to get involved with a reading program in an underprivileged area. Individuals signed up to volunteer not only to read to the children in a particular apartment complex every week, but to present them with a book to keep for their own at the end of the session. After a child had attended a certain number of gatherings, they were presented with a tabletop bookshelf bearing a plaque with their name on it that had been lovingly handcrafted by the volunteers.

The shelf is an excellent idea to present to your own child! What a great way to get them to understand that books are important—and so are they—and that they're both worthy of a shelf of one's own.

182. SHUFFLING THE DECK

BEDTIME

(Provided by Renee Barker)

   If we commit to seek solutions, we will find them.

My kids are seven years apart and were always at such different stages in development that I had trouble figuring out a good "one size fits all" bedtime routine to suit us. The eldest, a son, was allowed to stay up later than his younger sister but she still wanted someone nearby while she fell asleep. Reading aloud to him only kept her up later, asking questions.

One night we tried playing cards. My son was thrilled to show off his math and strategy skills and my daughter was able to get herself to sleep listening to the murmur of our conversation and the quiet slap-slap and shuffle of the cards. I heard more about school and friends during those card games than I ever heard at mealtime or in the car. I would tuck a new deck into his Christmas stocking or Easter basket each year, and eventually he was teaching me new games he'd learned. Playing cards has also given him common ground with my parents, which was especially useful during the middle-school years.

Almost any game is a great way to connect the generations, but cards are so portable and offer the widest variety for skill levels and interests. Two decks of cards will get this family through any power outage, rainy vacation day, or reunion.

183. Shelter from the storm

There have been many books written that encourage us to create a sacred space in our homes where we can go to retreat, if you will. Some suggest setting up "altars" where we can worship or meditate; others simply instruct us to create a cozy, restful corner where we can think or read, undisturbed. The main point is that once you create this space, something in you is automatically triggered when you approach it, just like what happens when I touch the magic doorknob to my office, thereby unleashing my creative juices. (Okay, so it's glass and I bought it at a flea market for five bucks, but you'll never convince me it isn't magic and don't even try.)

Help your child create their version of that special retreat place (No, I'm not talking about a time-out chair here!) so that when they are perhaps overwrought and needing some space, they will instinctively know where to go before having to be sent to that time-out chair we aren't talking about. Their own shelter from the storm (read: *you*) when the going gets tough. It can be as simple as a chair painted their favorite color and decorated with stamps or what not, or as complicated as a fort or special desk.

184. Disconnection

DISCONNECTED

I watched a national TV show this morning that talked about boys and their hidden emotions. Things like bullying and anger were discussed. The topic encompassed concealed sadness and promoted the theory that we need to stop saying, "Boys will be boys!" and using that as an excuse to allow for cruelty. Parents were distraught over their son's behaviors; sons were pent up with low self-esteem and occasional thoughts of suicide. Some punched things—and people—to vent themselves. Others worked to not feel anything at all. Most felt that no one, from parents to school officials, gave a rip about them and their sensitivities or even took the time to defend them, understand them, or permit them to cry.

Let me say this: The phrase "disconnected from my parents," or something that meant the same, came up often. I don't need to say anything more.

185. FOLLOW THE LEADER

Bookstore shelves are filled with experts telling us how to do just about anything we want to do (along with much we frankly don't give a squat about). Most of the time I think parents mostly need to just learn how to ride bareback, by the seat of the pants, forgetting fancy equipment and ideas. Just ride close to the "animal," hugging with your whole self.

There are, however, books that truly have good ideas, thereby enhancing our journey on this earth in the family kingdom. (Of course I'd like to think the book you are now reading is one of them.) Some of those books deal with the array of ways our children learn, their personality types, and so forth. This can be important, especially when you have a child completely unlike yourself and you just seem to be lost at connecting. Understanding a different "type" in a broader sense can help you understand your child.

A friend of mine condensed these discoveries into practical usage like this: "Watch how your child talks with other children. If your girl or boy is a side-by-side talker, offer yourself as a side-by-side listener. If face-to-face is the style, follow suit."

186. MORE THAN A MOM

I was recently chatting with a friend who had experienced a deep amount of trouble in his life, including incarceration. When the going was tough, he said he often thought about things his mother, who is now deceased, had taught him when he was a young man. She'd raised him alone, having never been married.

One thing in particular he shared with me was how he valued her honesty about a portion of her life. She'd explained how she'd been attracted to a man, his father, had gotten physically involved with him, and became pregnant. What she taught him, he said, by openly telling him about her youthful desires and what it led to, was that "She was a woman. My mother taught me she was a woman." The reverence and tone in his voice when he spoke of her caused me to realize the power in letting our children know we are more than a mom, more than a dad. We are men and women, flesh and bone. I'm not talking just about sexual matters here, but earnestly sharing who we are apart from parenthood.

Long after her death, his connectedness with his mother, a woman, was powerfully evident.

187. PLAY FAIR

It's interesting how many times I've heard someone admit to growing closer with a parent after the other parent has died, almost as though one gate needed to close before another could fully open. Of course it's natural for one parent to be more gregarious and handy at connecting than another. But if you are that gregarious and connecting one, make sure that in your enthusiasm, activities, and bountiful connectedness you're not crowding out room for the other parent to plug in.

What? You say they don't seem interested or don't have time? Just back out a bit, open the space and see what happens. Maybe even go so far as to arrange opportunities and activities that don't involve you. (I heard that gasp!)

If you are the quiet one who allows the other one to keep the bonding fires burning, throw a few logs on the fire, however small they may be at first. Children develop from what they're taught and what they witness. If your child has two parents, make sure they understand they both desire to be actively involved in their lives.

188. STEP STUFF

BLENDED FAMILIES

When George and I married, I brought my 4-year-old son and remnants of a failed marriage with me. George, age 30, had never been so much as betrothed before. Boy did we have a lot of adjusting to do!

Of course one of the most strenuous aspects of our adjusting involved parenting Bret together. George, eyes wide open and with full responsibility assumed the role of active fathering since that role was available. I recall many times thinking that some of the speed bumps in the relationship between George and Bret were due to the fact George had never raised a child before. There were a few times when I'd find myself begrudgingly thinking, "If that was *your* son from the start..." And then we had a son together.

Wow, was *I* the one with something to learn! The same issues between George and Bret that used to make me grind were exactly the same grindabouts between George and Brian. It wasn't a stepparent thing at all. Instead, it was a guy-to-guy thing along with some personality clashes.

Step-parenting is challenging enough without the natural parent making it worse. Don't make assumptions. Hear me now: Do not make assumptions about a relationship that hits a few bumps; it has to find its way. Cut that other guy or gal some slack so you don't find yourself getting in between.

189. MORE THAN MAKING DO

A great way to connect with your kid is to take him or her out on a "date." There are no limits to creative possibilities for "date night" with your kids. Do something special. Do something more than pizza and an ice cream (although that's just ducky, too). For this particular mother and son (or father and daughter) extravaganza, why not make it, well, an extravaganza! Make reservations at a ritzy restaurant (as far as your budget allows).

If it's a daughter you're datin', have Mom "do" her hair and nails or better yet, make a salon appointment for those girly girl things. If it's a son, slick him up, tie a perfect tie knot, order a boutonniere ...you get the picture! Go crazy with the accessories! (You might even split for a limousine!)

There's no reason you can't do this with same-sex parent and child. Call it "Girls' Glamour Night" or "The Manly Men's Outing." Not only will this be an evening to remember, but you will have created an opportunity to teach them formal etiquette. If you also treat them with formal dignity, you will have modeled to them that they are worthy to receive it. Oh sure, you can model worthiness without all the fluff, but why not just drip in it, once upon a parenting journey?

190. Left behind

I was attending an estate sale once where I stood in the unfamiliar kitchen. While I was looking through an old family cookbook, I had to choke back tears. Although I didn't know the people who had lived there, I learned about pieces of their lives and family names by carefully turning the pages of the battle-worn cookbook. Tucked inside tattered, printed and faithfully food-spattered pages were handwritten recipes. Recipes were listed, such as Aunt Mabel's Boston Cream Pie, Harriet's Corn Casserole, Cousin Sally's Jell-O Salad, or Mom's Stuffing. Measurements for ingredients had notations changing a quarter cup of this to a half cup of that. There were a few Xs through obvious failures. You could tell the family favorites by the buildup of food left behind in the pages.

Years of planning and stirring and chopping, feeding babies and bellies, and breaking bread together. Traditions passed down through the ages. Memories left behind...to be sold at an estate sale to strangers.

Teach your children to care about family recipes. Tell them details about what you remember Grandma doing in the kitchen. Allow them to help you while you plan, stir, chop, and bake. Bake bread together, break bread together, digest family importance and history—together. The family cookbook deserves a sacred place in your home.

191. Towering trees

As I look out my second-story office window, the top of the front-yard blue spruce rises high above me. Planted 30 years ago, it came in a one-gallon bucket. It was so small in the beginning that we had to put a stake next to it to keep from mowing it down and to protect it from romping children.

We have pictures of it when it grew a bit bigger, amply circled by one flat of perky pink and white petunias. We laugh and marvel when we look at those old photos of that tiny green baby and then cast our eyes out the front window. It now spans a good portion of the front yard and towers like a sentinel. A beacon of strength, solidly defending our entire estate while gently sheltering the fragile birds who live in its strong boughs. It is as old as our youngest son.

Recently a friend talked to me about the angst of their upcoming move while showing me their latest photos. Of all the things they fretted leaving behind, one of the most difficult objects to wave goodbye to was the tree they'd planted years ago in honor of their daughter. She pointed to it in the photo, eyes clouding over. It, too, held the front-yard place of honor. Too big to move; too important to forget.

Look around you. What are some of the "markers" of your family? Talk about them with your kids.

192. The senses

I have very warm and distinct memories of brushing my mom's hair. Oh how she loved for me to brush her hair, arranging it this way and that. Clipping it up and back. Making her first look intentionally ridiculous and then transforming her into my young version of glamorous—which was probably still ridiculous but she never let on to me.

I recall rubbing my dad's bald head. Feeling the slightly oily texture. Noticing the smell of manufacturing oils that clung to his clothing after work like a familiar friend that followed him home every night.

Touch. Yes, it is good to hug your children and comb and brush their hair. But what will they remember about touching you? Holding hands? Snuggling close? The fragrance you wear? Are you still enough for them to find out?

193. Thank you

It's a wonderful thing to be thanked and appreciated. Not that everything we do should be praise oriented, but I can't imagine many adults who aren't fueled to keep on keepin' on by a sincere and simple "Thank you!" or "Good job!" or "I'm glad you're on my committee."

Just remember that children are really just mini-adults without as much experience. (I heard this phrase on television lately and it really rang true.) They, too, are fueled by the same categories of things that float our boats, stroke our egos, and encourage us to volunteer again.

Catch them doing something right then thank them for it. Thank them especially if it was something you didn't ask them to do, (such as them sitting quietly for five minutes, picking up a toy, being nice to someone, whatever). And if you're going through a period where you don't think your child *doesn't* do anything right, look again. But look with careful eyes only watching for the positive.

194. THINKIN' 'BOUT YA

I travel quite a bit for my job. When I'm on the road, I usually phone my husband every night so we can bring each other up to speed regarding the day's foibles, adventures, and victories. Occasionally I phone my sons if I discover something I believe to be of special interest to them. I recently phoned Bret from my cell phone when I was standing in Woodstock N.Y., expressing how I just knew he'd enjoy a long motorcycle ride through the lush Catskills. I wished he was there to share the fun moment with me: stunning scenery, artistic community types, leftover hippie dudes, fun stories, and more.

Upon my arrival home from another trip shortly afterwards, I was greeted by my usual: a beeping answering machine. I sighed, gathered my note pad and pen, plopped tiredly into the chair and readied to chronicle the latest list of who needed what from me. To my glorious surprise, amidst the tasks was a message that set my sails.

"Hi Mom!" It was the happy voice of Bret. "We're 750 feet deep in the Carlsbad Caverns and we thought we'd call you for a change to tell you where we are. Here's Brian."

"Hi!"

"Hi!"

"Hi!"

"Bye!"

"Bye!"

A quick and humorous, chirping volley between them let me know my sons, vacationing together, were having a good time and thinking about me. I left it on the machine for days, just to play it again and again when I needed a lift.

Whose spirits aren't lifted by learning they're being thought about? Whether it's daycare, vacation, or the backyard, take time, via note, phone call, or holler to connect.

195. DISCOVER AND DONATE

It's liberating to free yourself from some of your own junk. Clear out the clutter—or shovel out the debris—if you're really in a bad way. We get so fried about our kids' rooms without giving too much thought to the fact that they just have too much stuff in them—rotten food, underwear, socks, and crumpled up paper aside. I'm talking about the fact that we all have too much stuff.

In order to help encourage cleanliness and benevolence in the same shot as well as work on a project together, have a few days in the year when you clear it out. A family "Discover, Dump, and Donate Day," perhaps. Make posters and hang on the fridge and bathroom mirrors warning—err, I mean advertising—when these days will arrive. Begin talking ahead of time about how good it will feel to lighten up the entire family's load. Plan dinner out the day of the drop off, thereby lending an air of celebration rather than chore to the upcoming event. (How about Donate and Donuts Day?)

Have everyone submit ideas for the charity of their choice. In our area we have several resale shops, each benefitting a different organization. They range from family services, to mental illness, to the Salvation Army. If you decide to have a garage sale at the end of your clean up instead, organize the troops, assigning duties and shifts. Perhaps you could donate the money to a charity, or at least a portion or prearranged percent of it.

196. LEND ME YOUR EAR

Sometimes the best way to get reconnected with your child is to get reconnected with yourself. If you are in a frustrated period— say on the verge of hysteria—then it's time to talk to somebody. Perhaps it's another parent, one who's been in the trenches. Tell your stories. Share your pent up (or spewing-out-your-mouth) anger. You'll find if you share your stories with honesty, even the ones that embarrass you the most because you think you're the only one who's ever experienced them, you'll undoubtedly learn you are not the only one who's experienced them. You will have also freed whomever you talk to tell you about their trials.

It's actually funny how quickly the one-upmanship game can be launched. Before you know it, laughter has jiggled your frustrations down into a manageable pile, thereby readjusting your attitude back into a perky, parental managing mode. Okay, maybe perky's expecting too much. But better is good, right?

197. SEIZE THE PRE-MOMENT

Occasionally we find ourselves blindsided by the flaring heat of a battle with our children that arises out of nowhere. (Well, at least we think it's nowhere.) I mean, how could they want to wear something that looks like that? Surely we've talked about family propriety and those boys (pointing and wagging our fingers all the while) look ridiculous wearing those pants falling off their behinds. And *oh my gosh* those girls look like street walkers. Then we take our own children shopping and shazam—we are dumbfounded at their terrible taste and obvious lack of memory. After all, haven't we covered this topic before?!

Perhaps *we* haven't discussed it at all. Perhaps we've just *ranted*. Perhaps our blind judgment and strong opinions haven't left any room for our child to learn to think through these things themselves because they're so busy blocking verbal arrows flying fast and furious.

Some time when you're all watching television together, driving in a car, or doing anything anywhere (as long as calm talk is prevailing) where your version of "questionable" crosses your paths, ask your child what they think of that attire, hairdo, or whatever. Tone of voice is everything here. Ask if they think the behavior or dress is symbolic of anything. Ask if their friends are dressing like that (not "like *that*"). If you engage these types of discussions frequently when the air is calm, you might have a chance—in the course of dialogue—to help your child consider dress and behaviors in a different light. Perhaps you'll even learn something so astounding that you'll change *your* mind about what matters.

198. TIME TOGETHER

You say your children are fighting and arguing and making you crazy? You say you're sick and tired of being sick and tired of it? Well, here's a hint I once heard that makes total sense: Send them to the "time-out chair" together (or couch, area, corner, or whatever— there is no end to the possibilities I've seen). They have to sit there, side by side, until they can apologize, hug, and depart in calmness and kindness. One person told me her kids even have to hold hands. It doesn't matter who started it, they have to solve it.

How does this connect *you* with your kids, you ask? You will have demonstrated that you value peace amongst family members. And here's how to take it a step farther: send yourself and your child there when you've squared off with one another. Perhaps a little "time out" time together would help bring you clarity as well. And by the way, hold hands. And if the temptation to squeeze their little fingers off seems impossible to stifle, immediately go lock yourself in the bathroom until you are calm.

199. HOLIDAZES

There are national holidays that will astound you. Did you know there's a National Pickle Day, Egg Salad Week, and Siblings Day? There's even—and I heard this on national TV this very morning—a National Take Your Dog To Work Day! There are books and calendars that note anniversaries of important events in history (such as the day Teflon was invented).

If you're searching for large and little things to celebrate, and/or plan an outing or adventure around, load yourself up with a few of these resources. Your local bookstore or library will be glad to direct you. Make the resource finding its own adventure. Let your children pick out what they think is worth celebrating. Then do it!

200. Think about it

"Most people are about as happy as they make up their minds to be." —Abraham Lincoln

Think about it long and hard. Then share the statement with your children. In fact, paste it on your refrigerator door, the inside of your medicine cabinet, your mirror, your kitchen windowsill, your bedroom nightstand, and the back of your eyeballs.

201. The art of play

Because I speak at parenting events, I have ample opportunities to dialogue with parents and hear their concerns. Some of them don't know how to play and therefore they don't know how to play with their kids who keep asking them to do so.

Many childhoods have been fraught with unkindness, alcohol, or events and behaviors that kept youngsters on full alert rather than being relaxed and open to creative outlets. And now these children are the parents, wanting something different for their kids.

So how do you play? First off, give yourself permission to do so. Tell yourself, convince yourself, that this play time will neither be wasted time nor unproductive time because play is important for balance, connection, and perspective. (Perhaps define the time as 15 minutes and actually set your timer so that you know when your discomfort zone will end.) In allowing our minds to tap into possibilities, we find answers to questions that keep us bound up and feeling isolated, dull, and stuck.

Let go, for at least five minutes, of the idea that everything has a place and everything should be in its place. (I know this is causing some of you to hyperventilate but stay with me here.) Being messy is good for play.

Grab a bag of cookies, untuck your shirt tail, get down on the floor, and drive a toy truck, making your best possible truck noise (mine stinks, but it doesn't matter). Drive the truck to wherever your imagination takes you. Don't have an imagination? Drive to your last vacation spot.

It's a beginning.

Give yourself permission to watch *Mr. Rogers' Neighborhood*, who is a master at play and pretend. See him as your teacher. He will guide you. Be the child. Watch the child. Copy the child. Learn.

202. THE BEAUTY OF A MESS

Forts made out of couch cushions and blankets. A basement floor filled with misshapen blocks of wood, nails, screws, and tools. Food coloring, flour and salt drizzled on the counter, evidence of experimental concoctions. An entire play town, set up across an entire living room floor: buildings, trucks, restaurant, garage, and all. Remnants of play and memories.

Order can and will prevail. But now is the time for messes.

203. SOMETHING NEW

I once signed up to take an adult, continuing education watercolor class (no credits, no pressure) so I could be involved in an activity that needed no words. It didn't matter that I have no artistic ability. (But what if I discovered that I *did?*) I just wanted to play with color and water, smearing, wondering, and playing. The teacher was perfect because she taught 8th grade (just my speed and attention span).

I wished my grown children were there taking it with me so we could oooh and ahhh over one another's creations. Or we could laugh or look totally confounded, whichever the case might produce. I wished I'd taken this class when they were small and that they were there with me. All of us there, learning something together; experiencing something new together. Something that peaked all our interests.

Golf. Bowling. Chess. Weaving. Archery. Italian food. What might *you* learn together in a class, video, or kit?

204. The golden smile

(Provided by Karin Baker)

My 4-year-old daughter, Brooklyn; my son, Austin, age 2; and I have decided that smiling just makes everyone feel better. Our golden rule for each and every day is to smile at five people. Whether they're people we know or strangers in the grocery store, a smile can make you and the recipient feel so good! We love to *smile*!

One particular day, after the workday was over and we were on our way home, Brooklyn asked if I had done my smiling for the day. Emotionally drained and worn out from the day, I told her that there was not much for me to smile at on that day. She looked puzzled, then responded. "Mommy, you have a picture of me on your desk don't you?" I answered yes. She continued, "When you don't have anything else to smile at, look at my picture and I will make you smile."

From that day on, when the work day is getting long and I have nothing to smile at, I look at my Brooklyn and smile from ear to ear. See, a smile can make anyone feel good.

205. Join in

Even if your child is still a baby or toddler, you'd be amazed at the number of resources you can scout up that enable you to exercise together. The local YMCAs have water aerobics classes for parents and tots. Video stores have tapes of just about every kind of exercise you can think of—from stretching to kick boxing. There are even workout routines using your baby as a weight for leg lifts, which keep them entertained and giggling. Mini trampolines about a yard in diameter are a welcome cardiovascular workout for those old enough to not take a header off the springy centers. (Are you?) Jump ropes. Sidewalks to walk upon. Chalk and sidewalks to create hop scotch templates.

Better health, sleep, and fun will prevail when you exercise together.

206. OVERTHINKERS

Growing up, I do not ever remember my parents saying, "Well what will people think?" What I would occasionally hear was, "What do you care what people think if you know it's right for you?"

What a wonderful gift that was. What a gift of grace to pass along to your children. It not only discourages peer pressure but also keeps them from becoming slaves to appearance. (Every time we bind them to what other people think, we are teaching them to cave into peer pressure.) They shouldn't run everything they do through the filter of onlookers who may judge them right into an unsatisfied, not fun, and boring life (much like the lives of those who find nothing better to do than judge the rest of us).

207. NEVER LOOK BACK

Every time we continue to carry on about a spilled glass of milk; a child who stays up too late and is crabby; a bad report card; a missed curfew; a selfish child who won't let another play with their toy; or whatever else we chose to continue being miserable about, we are sending a message. A message that says looking back is the way to go through life and misery is supposed to hang around.

Wait! There's another way! One that encourages and helps a child look forward to life. "Next time I'm sure you'll be more careful," or "Accidents happen," or "I'm sure this wasn't your best effort and I can't *wait* to see what happens when you really jump in next time," or "I know you are a kinder child than that last exhibit and I bet you'll find out how fun it is to share next time."

I am here to remind you that adults spill; I've seen it twice in restaurants, just this week. If a waitress came up and rode our backs for an hour afterwards, we wouldn't stand for it. Neither should our children have to. Accidents happen. Adults knowingly stay up too late. Adults don't always treat people fairly. But we forgive ourselves and move on. At least I sure hope we do.

When I left my father's house for the last time after his death, I was weeping. I was having a difficult time tearing myself away from this last place of memories and fighting the urge to turn around and hurl myself back into the house during my final walk down the sidewalk in the side yard. Then in my head and heart I heard his voice. I distinctly heard his voice and his familiar words. "Never look back. Down the road."

Responses to the small things ultimately feed how we handle the larger moments in life. Thanks Dad. Thanks.

208. TANGIBLE TIME

On Mother's and Father's Day, newspapers are filled with essay contest winners. "My mom is the best because," or "My dad should win because." The reasons children give for their parent being the best is based on the tangible time they spend with them. I couldn't help but see a pattern in every essay I read:

- "My dad gives the best hugs."
- "He is so busy but he still finds time to..."
- "He tells me about things."
- "Mom bakes my favorite cookies."
- "Mom plays cards with me."
- "Mom taught me how to change the oil on my car."

Very seldom have I ever seen any of them talk about how much money their parents spend on them. Or how they have the biggest, best whatever. Or that their parents drop them off at the most lessons or games. Their parents "rock" because they give, help, hug, talk, and teach.

Spend some tangible time with your children today. Who knows, you may see their appreciation published in the newspaper!

209. A TOE HUG

(Provided by Alan Harris)

Whenever the opportunity presents itself and by whatever means available, seize the moment to express your love. It is never too late or too complicated.

My father Keith was about to undergo brain surgery to remove a cancerous tumor. He was always a witty but stern parent to me, and we grew to carry several "no-man's-lands" between us where we just couldn't understand each other. By all that he did and provided for us, I knew well that he loved me and my siblings. But he was by no means an "I love you" sayer, nor was he demonstrative with hugs, being emotionally reticent behind his daring wit.

After Dad, then 60, was made comfortable on a gurney, ready for cartage into the operating room, Mom and his children wished him well. When it came my turn, I told him he deserved to come out of this surgery with all of his faculties, even though the 1928 piano lessons might go down the drain. For the first time I could remember in my 37 years, he said "I love you." I told him I loved him too. The path to his head was obstructed by other people, so I squeezed his big toe as a hug. The surgery was successful but unfortunately it was only a stopgap, and he died a year later—but not without our having told each other with voices and toe what we never could before.

210. FEEL THE RUMBLE

George and I went to the stock car races last night. We do this at least once every summer because we both enjoy them and I'll whine if we don't. I love stock car races, but I do not like Indy cars because the cars don't rumble. Stock cars, Harleys, and broken mufflers rumble, and that, if you are me, is an exciting sound. This is no doubt a learned behavior—although I'd really like to think it was passed on through the genes of my mother who for weeks would put off getting the tailpipe on the car fixed because she loved bombing around in the rumble, revving.

Together we'd go to the grocery store and Mom—knowing her daughter also loved this earthy, vibrating sound—would gun the car and we'd both grin and squeal till we thought we'd explode. It was like our personal clandestine escape into the "wild life." Then we'd slowly, very slowly, eke up the driveway so Dad didn't hear it quite so loudly and ask why Mom hadn't taken it in yet.

Now I am not advocating air pollution (and this was back in the days before we were this smart ecologically). But I am advocating this: Find the thing that you and your child like to do that feels solely yours. The thing that you both can't wait to steal away to do together.

211. WHEN OTHERS SPEAK

I am always running across quotes that speak to me. Good quotes inspire, ignite, appropriately convict, teach, impregnate our souls, and keep giving. I have added them onto my computer so that one of my favorites pops up first thing each morning. I have them taped and nailed and stuck to my office walls. I have them memorized; I pass them on in speeches.

Start a favorite family quotes scrapbook, cork board, or refrigerator corner. Teach your children to have eagle eyes to pluck them from paragraphs. Have everyone write them down along with the date they learned of it and the source from which they retrieved it. (I wish I'd have been smart enough to do this with some of my favorites!) Each month, bring together all the new ones family members have gathered and share them. Discuss why they mean something to you. Whether wise, funny, ridiculous, or completely incomprehendable, sharing your favorite quote will also share your priorities, tastes, and much more. Coincidentally, here's one of my favorites; I bought it on a plaque: "Never try to teach a pig to sing...it wastes your time and annoys the pig." Right on!

212. BLENDED JUST RIGHT

BLENDED FAMILIES

If you have a blended family, make sure you are careful to honor *both* families. Whether the child is arriving for visitation or returning afterwards, for him or her to feel like they need to leave a favorite ritual, passion, or *parent* on the doorstep when they enter is a severe bruise to the heart. These feelings of hurt can perhaps become insurmountable between the two of you. At the very least—and at the painful most—it might fill that tender child with consuming guilt simply for continuing to love the other parent or stepparent when your ire is so obvious.

If you find yourself wishing the child *didn't* love that other person, and perhaps even outwardly voicing opinions to turn them away from a mother or father or stepparent, get some counseling. Now. To overtly poison any relationship between a parent and child or to breathe darkness into a home is *wrong*.

I realize there are situations where parent and child need to be separated for real reasons, such as abusive relationships. However, I'm talking about keeping your personal wounds, jealousy, and vindictiveness from spreading where it doesn't belong. You need to keep your child from becoming a pawn in an emotionally unhealthy game.

213. HIT YOUR KNEES

Sometimes the goin' gets tough and it is easy to lose perspective, hope, and patience. Cecilia Wall knows what that was like; she fought and fought with her daughter when she was in high school. "Now we're *so* close," she says. In fact Cecilia is nothing short of a large part of her daughter's own family now.

She says the way to stay connected when things get bad is to do a lot of praying. Pray God will guide the child and give you patience. Try to understand what is going on in this young child's life.

"Really," Cecilia says, "she wanted independence and it was just pretty hard to cut those ribbons."

214. MORNING RITUALS

I received my first pedicure not long ago. In the course of the wandering conversation between me and the pedicurist, I received one of life's important instructions: After a shower, dry thoroughly between each toe. The pedicurist explained, "Slow yourself down and run the towel between each toe with deliberate strokes. This is a good way to help ward off funguses of all kinds; you'd be amazed, once you think about this, how often we don't take the time to really dry between our toes. We just skim across the top and bottom of each foot." I tested her theory my very next shower. She was right; I was a skimmer.

In my entire life I can only remember having athlete's foot twice. And I now have just the teensiest beginnings of a toenail fungus on one toe on one foot. (I know what you're thinking; too much information!) But the point of all this gross stuff is this: It's amazing how much of life we skim through, including the details about our children.

If your kids are still at an age when you dry them after a shower, remember to dry carefully between each of their toes. Who knows what you might ward off...as well as discover about them during that close and methodical ritual, way beyond their feet! If your child already dries him or herself, pass on this pearl of wisdom. And just for the heck of it, give your own piggie drying a wee little test, "all the way home."

215. SAY IT ON PAPER

If you have a tendency to explode or launch into "Lecture Number 47"—you know, the one that begins, "If I have told you once I've told you a thousand times!"—make yourself write it down. Don't just spew out complaints. When you yell instead of write, that nasty and dishonoring tone of voice is harnessed and clarity without hysterics can prevail.

Perhaps by the time you've written your complaint down, you will have diffused yourself, and whatever it was won't even seem very important any more.

216. ONE AND ONLY

When Bret was heading toward the end of his high school days, he received a report card that just didn't "sing," to put it lightly. (At least it didn't "sing" anywhere near the tune I'd been hoping for.) Because his report card came in the mail during the middle of the day, it gave me time to realize I needed to write a note to express my feelings, rather than fuel up for a verbal attack when he walked in the door. (I can be very good at this and it is never pretty.) On a yellow legal-sized piece of paper, on one side I wrote, "Who Am I?" On the other side I wrote, "My goals and how I plan to achieve them." I figured he'd be in his room for hours contemplating tough issues after he saw his report card. And so I settled in to wait.

No longer had I fixed myself an iced tea when he emerged from his bedroom, handed me the paper and disappeared out the door. On the "Who Am I?" side he had written, "I am Bret Haskins, the one and only." As for his goals, they included living near the mountains, having a job he liked, owning a dog, having good friends, etc. He has more than achieved them all. Much more. He knew exactly who he was. However, it was I, his one and only mother, who was confused.

Deep inside your child rests your child's very own answers. Don't assume *you* know what they are. The task is to help them discover them for themselves. Perhaps all they need is a question.

217. DREAMS DO COME TRUE

I often hear parents, when asked what their child is studying in college or pursuing in their lives as they near adulthood, say, in as disgruntled a tone as one can muster, "What does it matter. They want to be a drummer in a rock band (or an actor or movie producer)." The parents then sigh, roll their eyes in disgust, and spend their time inciting their "naive" child's light to finally dawn. (This is the light that beams the headline announcing: "You're not going to make a living *that* way, doofus!")

I also often hear famous movie producers, recording artists, actors and actresses, and novelists say, "I knew from the time I was a child that this was what I was going to be." Remember that next time you're sighing and learn to honor your children's dreams. For all great achievements to happen, the dream must come first.

And while you're in the business of honoring dreams, what is yours? I once heard some profound words on this topic: "*It's never too late to become what you might have been.*" Amen.

218. MONTHLY MEETINGS

(Provided by Susan McCullen)

> *Our children learn to honor
> what we teach them is of value.*

My 17-year-old daughter and I reserve Friday nights once a month for just the two of us. It's our "movie marathon night" and we'll rent four or five movies. Some are her choice, some are mine, and some are mutually agreed upon. We stock up on our favorite snacks and drinks, order dinner out (say, pizza, or swing by the KFC), close the doors, ignore the phone, and snuggle in for the night.

We giggle, laugh, cry, and discuss together. It is a great bonding time. We both comment on the movies, what we liked, what we didn't, what was good, what was bad, which ones we would see again, which we would like to buy, and which to never waste another moment on. Many times the subject matter of the movies will bring on wonderful conversation about how it relates to our own lives or the lives of those we know. Conversations sometimes continue for days afterward. I love the closeness we share and how much closer we become when we do this. It helps us to both see another side of the other so often missed in daily exchanges.

I realized just how special this time was to her one night when her friend called in the middle of a movie. She asked her friend to call her back the next day because this was our marathon night.

219. LAUGH YOUR TROUBLES AWAY

Heard a good joke lately? Do something so stupid that you had to laugh at yourself? See a cartoon that cracked you up? Pass it on to your kids then ask them what tickled their funny bone today. Encourage encounters with laughter. Be deliberate in modeling that gift. Shared laughter diffuses tension and can be a transition to forgiveness and literally help us heal and live longer. Cultivating and keeping a sense of humor is, I believe, one of the primary principles of parenting. And as the Good Book says, a merry heart is a good medicine.

220. THE BEST FOR LAST

BEDTIME

(Provided by Linda Burke)

Our ritual began when my husband started a landscaping business in addition to his primary 9-to-5 job as an engineer. The demands of his schedule made time with the kids scarce, at best. It was not unusual to find him eating dinner at 9 p.m.

One night he crawled into bed with our youngest and she said, "Daddy, tell me about your day." Fighting exhaustion, he attempted to skim over the surface and leave out the details. She interrupted him and said, "No, I mean tell me everything. And then I want to tell you about my day."

Bedtime and tuck-in time evolved into a nightly habit of sharing and connecting with our children. The bedroom is a place of serenity at the end of the day. The room is dark, and only the hum of the fan disturbs the quiet. We slip under the covers and hold each other—legs too! In those moments just before sleep we tell each other about our day. Even our 14-year-old son enjoys these special moments alone—one-on-one—with Mom and Dad.

Our children know that no matter how crazy our lives may be, they can count on us to listen, talk, and hold them before the day is through. They know that we save the best for last.

221. GOAT-GETTER OR GIFT

Brian was a stubborn child...and I mean *stubborn*. I'm surprised I have a nose hair left in my nostrils because plucking them often seemed easier and less painful than trying to get that child to cooperate. (Yes, sometimes it was that bad!)

Today, that child—just like his daddy—is an engineer. Stubborn people make good engineers because nothing will happen until they say whatever they're working on is ready to work, perfectly.

Engineers cannot be spontaneous activators, like Bret and I. (We'll think later, clean up the mess later, whatever later, but right now we are *activating!*) Brian and my husband are methodical people, calculating, measuring, planning, procedure-driven...

Is your child an activator or calculator? Remember, it takes both kinds to keep the world running (activator) smoothly (calculator). If your child shows a frustrating and extreme tendency toward either of these modes, consider this: Your job is not to break their natural inclination; it is to aim it.

222. RECEIVE THE LESSONS

In a completely uncharacteristic moment, my teenage son popped off to me with words that stung. His comments were biting, and seemingly flew out of left field.

"I can't believe you said that to me," I said incredulously. I was stunned and desired to lash back. Before I could utter another word, he spoke again.

"You talk to Dad all the time that way lately," he said flatly and without blinking. We were now standing nearly nose to nose. In an instant, I knew I had heard the truth. I'd heard the power and truth of the voice of God come out of the mouth of my son. I stood convicted.

Pride and ego would have lashed back. Grounded him. Smacked him. Made excuses. Gone into denial. Blamed the tiredness and busyness of my life—whatever struck first. But through a giant dose of undeserved grace, humility helped me own up to the truth and receive the lesson. It was time to become accountable for myself and I was very grateful for the courage of my son who helped me see the error of my ways.

Listen to your kids. They know stuff.

223. SATURDAY MORNING MUGS

I don't drink coffee, but I watch people flocking to the gourmet coffee stores ordering their "triple whammy double dribble doodah" coffees. As I watch them, I realize that more than the taste, or the caffeine, it is the familiar ritual of getting the special coffee that brightens them. (Okay, caffeine counts, big time, but there's much more to it than that.) Life can get so hectic that simple icons of modus operandi can be a warming, welcoming thing for families, too.

Make a trip to a store that sells mugs. Have each family member, including yourself, purchase one that feels just right (just like baby bears' bed). Right size handle. A depth that makes sense. (Thin and tall mugs keep things warm longer, but short and wide just feels better in some people's mouths.) Right colors. Right everything.

Then designate your mug to be your Saturday or Sunday morning mug. (Although it could be whatever day you choose.) Don't use them unless they and you are entering a "no stress, no hurry zone" in your day. Much like the triple whammy double dribble doodah coffees, seeing your mug as you whip through hectic workaday mornings may remind each of you of the promise of good things to come. Then make sure they do.

224. ACTING THINGS OUT

I recently keynoted at a young authors' conference to 500 third through fifth graders. Because my baby is 30, I sat in on a fifth-grade class beforehand so I could be reminded (or learn, in this century) exactly what kids are like at that age. What I learned by observing on a day when they were acting out mini-plays they'd written was that they really welcome interaction and that they have refreshingly fertile imaginations. As I put my talk together, I kept those things in mind.

At one point in my presentation I had volunteers come up on the stage. I gave them each a piece of paper with a scenario on it, along with props readied. One time I had a girl wear a makeshift wedding veil. (Of course the kids hooted and hollered and loved that one!) I had she and the "groom" approach one another and then I had the groom act like he fainted. I then asked the kids what they thought happened. The array of possibilities was amazing!

Resurrect the old game of pantomime. The guesses will give *you* a clue as to where all your child's mind can wander. Besides, the time spent together will have been deliberate, lively, and fun.

225. TUB TIME

When babies are old enough to actually sit and play in the bathtub (rather than those plastic baby tubs) consider the bathtub ritual prime connecting time. Rather than steeling yourself up for the tussle and mess, shift your attitude to one of joy-filled anticipation. Get the toys. Ready the fluffy towel. Sing the "Rub A Dub Dub" song or make up your own splash and drip tune. You and your spouse (yes, both of you) get down on your knees (cushioning with towels or something so you can get back up again) and play, sail, scrub, and rinse away. So what if you get splashed. You won't melt.

And don't forget to dry between those toes. No, don't forget that.

226. THE WHOLE ENCHILADA

(Provided by Mikki Nelson)

My preteen son and I like to take a whole day and find things to do together. Usually we start out going to the antique malls and begin looking around in there. This gives us the opportunity to learn some things about the past that we maybe didn't know. It also gives us a chance to see the different types of things that uniquely interest us, such as Ricky's penchant for fossils and different types of sports cards. (Oh and let's not forget Beanie Babies!!)

Later in the day we may go bowling. It's a lot of fun and it gives us both a chance to teach each other something. Ricky will make suggestions on how I throw my ball; I can make suggestions on how he approaches a lane. This time also gives us space to talk about things in his life in a nonconfrontational way. Instead of Mom prying into his preteen business, it's just Mom and Ricky having a great time, talking about what's happening in our day-to-day lives.

By the end of the day we hit the movie store and find a movie we both would like to see and come home to curl up on my bed and watch the movie. This also serves as good time to snuggle. I play with Ricky's hair or give him a foot rub. It seems to help him wind down and relax before its time to get some sleep.

I really cherish these times with him. I think when I'm an elderly woman that these days, these activities we shared together, are what I'm going to most enjoy looking back on.

227. You started it!

Before our emergence into the bliss of fake-trees, our family piled into the car for our annual Christmas tree buying war. I'd like to use the word "extravaganza" or "adventure" rather than "war," but somehow we always managed to get in an argument. ("The tree is too fat, short, tall, expensive, crooked, ugly, whatever.") Or we'd freeze to death because it was the coldest day of the year and all trees were frozen shut like a turkey's butt when you're wanting to stuff it.

One year we actually discussed how we would try and do better. We forced smiles on our faces—the little bits of them we could see because we were so bundled up—and piled in the car. About half way to the first lot (and we usually had to visit several), George broke out singing, in his relatively tuneless but jolly way, a made-up song that went something like, "We're off to get a Christmas Tree, a Christmas Tree, a Christmas Tree. Fa, la la, la la." Well we all broke out laughing, for a number of reasons. (Not the least of which was that bursting into song was out of character for George.) Every year afterwards, we would, at some point in our tree-buying adventure, either bring that incident up or break out into that silly song.

Music soothes the savage beast, so they say. Perhaps creating your own family song for whatever the occasion can become one of your family favorites...and help keep the battle at bay.

228. GRAB BAG

Throughout my growing-up years, whenever we'd be in a store that sold grab bags, my parents bought me one. We didn't come across them that often, but when we would, I could be assured of a mystery-for-a-moment entering my life. Yippie!

I would stand and look at all the bags (sometimes boxes), picking them each up, thinking about the weight and possibilities, imaging what treasures might be coming my way by perusing the rest of the goods in the store. I cannot remember a single, specific treasure, but I do know that all in all, I probably came out about even—from good stuff to questionable stuff. At the very worst, I surely didn't need whatever it was, but someone probably did and I would give it away or donate it to a local, fund-raising resale shop.

I've followed this same tradition with my sons, even occasionally having Santa give them one now. Together we laugh, anticipate, and discover. What more can you ask for under five bucks? (Sometimes you even get candy!)

229. STEP BY STEP

"Take a hike, buck-o!" Literally. But do it with your child. Walking is a calming, cardiovascular-building opportunity to talk about things that might not otherwise crop up when you're sitting face to face, deliberately attempting to learn what's new from your child. Sites and strolling present conversationally meandering opportunities.

230. STITCHED TOGETHER

My friend Larry Turner described a weekend that stitched his "fragmenting, grown-up family" together for one more weekend. As sons, wives, and grandchildren were gathered together, they passed squares of fabric up the stairs in pairs, then in strips, then in pairs of strips, up to the sewing machine where his wife, Donna, sewed them. Then back down the production line they came to their places in the design. At 2 a.m. the quilt was complete.

What a great vehicle for connecting for any family, including your extended family. All you need is one person who can run a sewing machine to make a simple, no frills, big-squares, family quilt. Have everyone bring (or send to someone's home, if you're scattered around the country) either a remnant of material from a fabric store, or better yet, have them select an old favorite article of clothing that's ready for the dust bin. Duties can be divided between cutting, arranging, and sewing. You can even farm the sewing out if no one owns a machine.

Beauty and perfection isn't the goal. The goal is binding together pieces of your family's life. And what a wonderful gift for the patriarch or matriarch or anyone's family who is ill, to find themselves wrapped in the efforts and "fabric" of their entire family!

231. ONCE REMOVED

Much like a relative who we would describe as once removed, many grandparents are as "removed" as well. I do realize many are serving in grandchild-rearing roles. (Perhaps some of them are reading this book.) But what most grandparents are once removed from is 24-hour a day care. I believe this to be the biggest reason each new grandparent echos the words of nearly all who have gone before them, "Being a grandparent is wonderful! It's everything you've heard and more. If I'd have known how wonderful it was, I would have been a grandparent first!"

I think the second reason they find it so blissful is that they are seasoned professionals. They learned what doesn't matter so they don't make issues out of everything. They have the wisdom of hindsight. Like the saying, "No one ever died from oven crud," they have the perspective to weed out what won't kill you and only go to the mat for what might.

Talk to the grandparents. Ask them what they fretted over as parents that they now wished they hadn't. Assume they have wisdom to impart because they've been around the block—*your* personal block. Know they are holding a key to joyful relationships with your kids. If your relationship with your parents was or is not a good one, perhaps asking these questions can help mend it. If that relationship is an impossible one, find some older mentors. Then learn from these once-removed folks whose gift is that of happy, relaxed connectedness.

232. Notes that stick

At the end of a small group session during a retreat I once attended, each person in the group had to write down one-word, positive attributes they'd noticed about each other. They wrote them on individual pieces of sticky-backed paper and we each stuck them on our shirts. Throughout the day we were cloaked in positive affirmations, some we had never imagined about ourselves. It was a powerful and empowering experience; I still have the tags.

Do this with your children and have them do the same with you. Why not purchase inexpensive T-shirts (or rummage through drawers for usable ones) and have them write the words/affirmations in indelible ink? Use different colors and date them. When anyone is having a bad day, including you, they can be worn as reminders that there is more than just the bad times or bad attitudes. You seeing them in their shirts will remind you that there's more to *them* than their bad sides, too.

233. Notice what you do right

When something you do turns out right, let your children hear you talk about it. Express satisfaction in knowing a job you did was well done. In doing so, you will have given them permission to do the same.

234. Snails and puppy dog tails

Not everyone desires to own a dog or cat. (Many can't due to allergies anyway.) But everyone—be they apartment dwellers or estate claimers—can have *some* kind of pet. The range is limit-less. Over the course of rearing our sons we had dogs, gerbils, hermit crabs, and fish. Each taught us something about them *and* ourselves, besides simple responsibility. Dogs, of course, extend unconditional love and listen to our children, even when we don't (and vice versa).

In fact, all pets have that capacity. Gerbils modeled cuddling (as well as what it looks like to be spinning our wheels). Hermit crabs taught us to pay attention to when we've outgrown our shells when it's time to seek bigger territory. The fish, well they taught us that you shouldn't put them in an uncovered dish pan when you're fully cleaning out their aquarium. The youngest sibling obliged them with an entire can of fish food in his attempt to "help feed the fish," and then left them on the floor in the dish pan. They leap out, unnoticed, and got squashed into smears by my husband's size 13 shoe. (The fish also taught us how to say goodbye before the flush.)

Pets. Have them. Study them. Talk about their lessons.

235. BINDINGS THAT TIE

Susan McCullen pulled a memory from her junior high school days that helped prison inmates connect with their families over the holidays. It is certainly an idea that translates to any family that finds themselves apart for special occasions, including families separated by divorce. This idea is simple: Make a family "What Christmas Means to Me" book (or a "What Your Birthday Means to Me," book—it works with any occasion).

Use a manila folder cut in half and held together with yarn for your binding. Each parent, child, or extended family member draws a picture and/or writes a poem or short story to share, one that expresses their sentiments. You can even include puzzles, photographs or pictures cut from magazines. Susan said one family added scrapbook type pages with photos of presents being opened along with scraps of the wrapping paper and ribbon. Be creative. The possibilities are limitless.

The person who creates the original binder can fill it with their thoughts and send it to the next one on the list (or whom they choose), who will add their pages and send it to the next until it returns to the one who will keep it. (Alternate version: Have everyone mail pages to one person.) Eventually, everyone's thoughts, wishes, and images will be bound together. The book will be a means of connection for a child (and/or yourself).

236. A CHOICE OF ONE'S OWN

(Provided by Donna Turner)

> *Sometimes we get our knickers in a knot over things not going the way we envision they should. Perhaps then, more than ever, is the time to loosen the grip a notch lest our children rebel against us and we all lose what is important.*

When our son Scott was 13 and his classmates joined the confirmation class in our church, Scott said he didn't want to take part. Our pastor, who was a left-handed rebel like Scott, was clearly hurt and asked Scott to join the class, even if at the end of the class he chose not to be confirmed. We asked the pastor throughout the year how things were going and made it clear that he didn't have to join the church if he didn't want to. This was a commitment he must make because he wanted to. Several weeks before Confirmation Sunday, Scott decided he was not ready to join the church. We assured him that was okay because he could change his mind anytime he wanted to.

My husband and I came home from shopping late Saturday afternoon before Confirmation Sunday to find Scott sitting at the kitchen table making a banner. "What are you doing?" we asked. We were both flabbergasted.

"I'm making a banner," was his reply. "We need to do that as part of the confirmation tomorrow."

"But you said you didn't want to be confirmed."

"I know, but I changed my mind."

The next day Scott went to the front of the church in his denim slacks and sport shirt, not a confirmation suit. But suit or no suit, he made the commitment on his own. To this day, our strongly independent son has remained a truly spiritual person.

237. WHAT'S FAIR

We are bombarded with reminders of things that go wrong in the world. From the reputation of countries to the lives of an individual who "went bad," nuances, facts, gossip, and people are played out, guessed at, spun, debriefed, debated, judged, sentenced, and strung before us. Rather than just fret and rant about them, use these conditions to engage in conversations with your kids. What do they think about a penalty suiting the crime? Was it fair? What do they base their opinion upon? When anyone wounds or shoots or kills, what are some of the things they think might have contributed to that behavior? Caution yourself from simply espousing your views or negatively knee-jerking to theirs. You might be surprised at what you hear.

238. BIRDS AND BEES

Who looks forward to giving "The Talk," aside from a sex education teacher? (And come to think about it, I've never asked them if they look forward to it either.) When to begin? How graphic to get? Is it ever too young? What if it's too late? Is talking about safe sex giving a wrong message? If I make consequences sound too terrible, will I mar them from enjoying one of the great pleasures of life? Do I dare be honest about my own experience? Do I *really* want to know about theirs?

If I don't talk about "it," will the idea of "it" just go away?

That's about the only thing you can count on that won't happen.

239. On being special

(Provided by Carolyn Armistead)

Every once in a while, if we have a free weekend or vacation day, we set it aside to be one child's special day. It's not a birthday or anniversary celebration; but a day to celebrate a member of the family, just because.

On a "Nikki Day," for example, Nikki is allowed to choose a morning activity, the lunch food and location (picnic or restaurant, for example), and an afternoon activity. There are limitations; only one activity can cost money (such as bowling, museum, or a movie), while the other has to be free (such as a walk by the river, a bike ride, filming our own home movie, whatever). The only other rule is that this celebratory day only involves the family.

We've been doing this for years; and although the activities change somewhat as the kids get older, the enthusiasm and joy of being "special" never wanes.

240. Who's the boss?

You are. Don't lose your authority and respect by mistaking any other role you might desire to lay for your children more important than pure and simple parent.

Who's going to be their boss one day? They are. Help them learn how to make decisions without you always being the boss. Yes, they'll make mistakes. We owe them the freedom to do that so they can learn how to recover from them. How else have *you* learned some of your most valuable lessons? How did you learn when it's time to be the boss?

241. Steal-away moments

A friend of mine recently attended a large social gathering with his family. During a steal-away moment, he and his young daughter stretched out in a hammock.

"As I laid there with her, looking in the only direction you could comfortably look—straight up—with her head resting on my out-stretched bicep, I spoke quietly to her, urging her to enjoy the beauty and silence of nature: the treetops, the squirrel's nest 'right up there', the blowing sky. Nothing else mattered," he wrote in an e-mail.

There are things to do, places to go, and people to see. And yet, in the midst of our hustle and bustle await golden steal-away mo-ments when nothing else will matter and all will be remembered. Expect them. Look for them. Find them. Seize them.

242. There's not enough time

(Provided by Michael Lewis)

Sometimes as I'm getting ready for work, there never seems to be enough time. I'm always running around (in no predictable or sensible order), getting dressed, assembling work papers, exercis-ing, eating breakfast, glancing at the paper, and so forth. No mat-ter how much time I've set aside, I always seem to be running late.

And it seems right as things are at their craziest, my eldest daugh-ter sleepily shuffles down the steps and says good morning with a hug and kiss. I could very easily remain in the craziness of ready-ing myself for the rat race, but as I see how fast she's growing, I've been consciously making an effort to include her, even in mun-dane rituals.

Why put my shoes on alone in the living room when I can sit with her in the den, and slip them on while watching *Sesame Street*? I must admit, it's a little difficult tying them snuggling with my arm around her, but somehow I manage. I could eat my cereal and sip my coffee alone in the kitchen, but I'd much prefer giving Sammy a few sips of coffee from the spoon—and I don't even mind when she mooches those tiny marshmallow bits from me. All she asks are for these little moments together as we both get ready to greet the day.

Our time with our kids is short. How can you change your daily routine to include them? Because before you know it, they'll be grown and on their own and then you'll have all the time in the world.

243. FUEL THYSELF

INTENTIONAL DISCONNECT

Good parenting takes insight, humor, patience, reserves, bravery, enthusiasm, and many other things that can be easy to muster when we're operating out of a personal overflow of energy rather than squeezing the sponge for that last drop. I can't think of one of those attributes of good parenting that isn't next to impossible to delve out when we're trying to give out of an empty bucket.

Whatever it takes to refuel yourself, make sure you're prioritizing time to get it, even if this means disconnecting from your kids for an hour, day, or week. Staying connected when you're empty is like mainlining numbness into your child's veins.

244. NEVER HURRY

An acquaintance of mine shared what she referred to as a life-altering secret she'd recently learned: "Never hurry," she said. "And then," I replied, pausing and moving my hand in a circle as though trying to get her to roll out the rest of the story. "That's it. Never hurry," she repeated. Looking at my watch, I explained how "interesting" that probably was to contemplate...but that I only had about 12 minutes to make my next appointment.

Several days later, like a mantra that activated itself, I heard her words ring into my head while I was speed showering and...suddenly became aware of the speed. Once I slowed myself down, I enjoyed the shower so much more. Water, suds, fragrance; everything else got done magically in the same amount of time as usual. That simple act caused me to ponder how quickly I move through many things in my life, like tasks—both fun and perfunctory—with my family.

Hurry doesn't make things get done quicker; it causes do-overs, bruises, and errors in judgment. It causes stress, crabbiness, and forgetfulness. Never hurry.

245. TASTE TEST

Next time you all go for ice cream at one of those places where they hand dip the scoops, have a sampling party. All those stores have cute little sampling spoons for your indulgence. Of course they might not be too happy if you wanted to taste more than a few, but get away with tasting as many as you can. Jump right in. Be brave and give another flavor a whirl. Don't be stuck in a rut. There are enough places in life where we parents need to remain steady; ice cream flavors isn't one of them. Cut lose when you can. Your kids will love it!

246. HAIRCUT WARS

Say you're in a war with your child over the cut, style, or color of their hair? Ah yes, I recall those days with my oldest son. He always wanted to wear his hair longer than I deemed appropriate. (Thank goodness I got over the shackles of all things "appropriate" before the second one came along!) Here's what God taught me about hair: In the grand scheme of things, it just doesn't matter. Personality traits, such as loyalty, honesty, and integrity grow in; bad haircuts and funky colors grow out. And to take that a step further, they fall out: That kid (now 35) with whom I fought about hair, is bald. Get the message there?

247. EMERGING ADULTS

When my oldest son got that "If I look real hard I can see it" moustache in late grammar school, I stubbornly didn't allow him to shave it. He was too young, I said. He'd have an entire lifetime to be shaving so why start too young? So I said no.

Hear me now: It was a dumb decision. The day he finally just shaved it—without permission and after much teasing from classmates—was a relief for both of us.

Puberty happens and your children change. Your daughters will have hairy legs. Moustaches will appear on your son's 6th-grade upper lip. Underarm straggles will pop up. When is your child old enough to shave whatever it is that needs to be shaved?

Well, here's a news flash: Hair grows. Whether you shave it or not, it grows. Whether you allow them to or not, hair will grow. The only thing that might be stifled by your stubbornly refusing to cave in to allowing the shaving of a few hairs is your relationship. Whether you are ready or not, they will mature.

248. HEART GIFTS

IN-LAWS

(Provided by Phyllis Ludwig)

> *When we truly welcome a daughter- or son-in-law into*
> *our lives, we welcome the piece of our child's heart that*
> *has been given to another.*

I learned how to be a mother-in-law from *my* mother-in-law who was a wonderful role model without even intending to be. When David and I were married, his mother gave me a photo album with snapshots of David—from his infancy to our engagement picture. I'll never forget how thrilled and touched I was at the time, nor how many times over these 37 years that I've studied those pictures. On the last page she wrote, "Only his mother could give you this most precious gift—a son."

That was the first of many generous and thoughtful gifts from this very special lady. But she also modeled an attitude of acceptance and approval for me. I'm convinced we didn't consistently raise our children with expectations that she always agreed with, but she never once made me feel criticized or devalued. Her way of imparting family values was to tell stories of her friends and their difficulties or problems with their adult children. It was a very effective strategy. We got the message.

When our son Michael was married, I lovingly made a picture album for my new daughter-in-law. And I believe she treasures her album as much as I treasure mine. I regularly remind myself of how good it felt to be loved and accepted for who I was and try to model what my mother-in-law modeled for me: gifts from the heart.

249. In the thick of it

When my boys were in school, every year I volunteered for something. Some years it was a weekly stint to the library where I either shelved books or worked on the computer with inventory. Some years I was "room mother," getting involved with class parties and field trips. Or I was "picture lady," or just worked in the cafeteria during the special hot dog days—the list goes on and on. I realize not every parent has the freedom to be involved in this way; I was a single, working mom myself for two years and I remember it well. But what I learned during my attendance was that all kids are squirrely. Life isn't easy when you're in school. My child was not unlike the others who were victims, mean themselves, left out, or king of the hill.

There are lots of ways to be involved with your child's activities after school, too. Coaching, scouting, YMCA activities, pee wee bowling—the choices are endless. Any time you can be in the thick of it for a reason—volunteering yet watching and observing—you have served a couple of purposes: You find out a bit of what their life is like and you show them you care about it.

250. Umbrellas from Heaven

(Provided by Jan Kwasigroh)

> *Sometimes angels unaware are treading in our midst.*
> *Sometimes we're even them. And to think, it's all*
> *because we pass something on!*

My husband was in the military and we were sent to the West coast—for the fifth time. This time, however, all three children would remain in the South at "the college of their choice." I remember getting a phone call one sunny day (a rarity in LA) from our daughter in Alabama. She asked me if I had sent her an umbrella. "No, I didn't." I replied.

"Well, I just got this bright yellow and white umbrella in the mail and, wait" —she must have been opening it— "it has an aspirin brand name on the bottom..."

"Wait!" I interrupted, laughing. "I bought several bottles some time ago and there was an offer for a free umbrella! I sent in the form with your name on it and forgot all about it! You're just now getting it?"

"Yes, but that's okay! And the funny thing is that I was in town yesterday and it really poured. I went to a fast food restaurant's drive thru to get a sandwich. As I left, I passed a guy pushing a small cart. He was homeless and trying to get under a bridge overpass about a half a block away. I pulled along side, rolled down my window and gave him my umbrella and my sandwich. He was very surprised and grateful. And now here today I have another one! Wow!"

251. NAMES OF ENDEARMENT

Bretski, My little Bri, Charstar, Sherbert, Bomb, Bigknee, Honey Bunny, Bomber, B-Man—all names of endearment for members of our family. Oh sure, there's Mom, Pop, Ma, Dad, Bret, Brian, Char, Charlie, and Good Old George. There used to be a Butch the Wonder Dog (may he rest in peace). Somehow there is an added level of intimacy, fun, and implied codes when pet names are used.

What are some of your family's pet names? Did you used to have a nickname when you were young? Share it with your kids and explain how you got it. Ask them if they've ever been called by nicknames at school and how they feel about them. What is their favorite name of endearment you use for them?

252. BLACK AND WHITE

When my brother and I were growing up, my parents occasionally used babysitters. (Thanks again, Mom and Dad, for modeling that was okay. You saved my own parental sanity!) Although we occasionally had a high schooler, more often we had one of two older ladies: Mrs. Goodwin or one other lady whose name I cannot remember. There is probably a good reason for that. We endearingly referred to Mrs. Goodwin—whether in her presence or not—as Mrs. Goodie. We groaned over the other one and didn't call her anything; we just glared back at her. They both wore black shoes with little dots of holes in them, thick stockings (too thick to call them nylons), and both were dressed plainly. One wore brightness and love on her face and the other looked perpetually tired and annoyed. One was as glad to see us as we were her; the other radiated the appeal of a splatted June Bug on the windshield. Perhaps life had not been kind to her, but she also made no attempts to make life pleasurable for those around her—at least when she was babysitting. She wasn't mean. She just wasn't much of anything other than there. She would watch, hawk, and wait to find something to tattle about.

When my parents would announce they were going out for the evening, we'd begin our high-pitched, hope-filled pleas with, "Is Mrs. Goodie coming?" We probably wore looks on our faces not unlike our family pet, Wonder Dog Butch, tongues hanging out, panting, heads cocked and looking ever hopeful a treat was soon coming our way. If the answer was affirmative, we'd cheer and run around like the little precious stupids we were. If the answer was no, we'd hold our breath in hopes anyone— anyone including aliens—was coming rather than old Mrs. Whatshername.

Point being this: On most days, a person(s) in charge of child care arrives with the same aura and to the same expectations as either of these two ladies. They are called "parents." Yes, you are what your child is stuck with. Try being Mr. or Mrs. Goodie.

253. I WONDER…

FEAR

"Curiosity will conquer fear even more than bravery will," author James Stephens wrote in *Crock of Gold*. What a great quote to help your kids conquer a daunting or unfamiliar task or road.

Rather than talking about how to look fear in the face, or telling them to just snap out of it, or get over it, or try to convince them it's really nothing, play the "I wonder" game and nurture their curiosity.

"I wonder what would happen if we _____."

"I wonder what would happen if you _____."

"If we didn't _____ I wonder how that would work?"

"What if you _____instead of _____?"

"I wonder how it feels to _____?"

254. Finding our way

Connecting with our children, bettering our relationship, trying again, starting over. Opportunities are limitless when our kids, no matter how old or young or near or far away they are, are alive. Even when we are estranged, hope, prayer, humility, and pursuit can often times bridge or close the gap. But when a child has succumbed to an early death or didn't make it into the world breathing, what then? How then do we feel connected?

Mike Lewis writes about a stillbirth, a boy his wife, Amy, delivered at 25 weeks into her pregnancy: "We had his ashes placed in the memorial garden of my church. Sunday afternoon we had a Spring barbecue there. The afternoon was winding down and I felt drawn to that memorial garden. I hadn't gone there in a while. It's beautifully landscaped, quiet, and there's a little bench there for reflection. I was sitting there, finding myself getting a little choked up, reflecting on what might have been." Mike's tender ponderings in the memorial garden included tending his own soul while contemplating telling his daughters about their "older brother" when they are one day old enough to understand.

I have had three miscarriages. I have friends who have lost teenagers. We grieve, we wonder, we laugh at memories, or wrench ourselves at those uncaptured or unlived. We celebrate the life that had courage enough to begin its journey into the world, whether your child arrived lifeless or was yours to love for decades on this earth...and forever in our hearts. And while lifting up the threads of life, laughter, and tears, we channel the passion into the opportunities and lives of those at hand.

255. FLY AWAY

When I was a child, the Cook brothers and I used to have a blast rummaging through the burnt garbage pile. (This was back in the days when suburbanites burned their garbage in their own backyards.) We'd find all kinds of exotic treasures like half melted and misshapen flash cubes (back in the days when cameras had individual, replaceable flash cubes), charred pieces of wood that looked like fins or panels of some sort, melted cans, and more. Fire had a way of transforming the ordinary into endless possibilities. Our imaginations were ignited by the treasures. We stuffed, glued, wired, and tied those things onto an old hot water heater behind the garage. It became our space ship and I'm here to tell you we left this earth, just like Flash Gordon. (Yes, I am that old.)

For the most part, we can't burn our garbage anymore, but we can certainly still go hunting for yesterday's stuff. Take your kids to resale shops, consider what you're tossing in the recycle bin, and keep your eyes peeled and your creative hats readied. Challenge them to make something for you out of 10 unrelated objects of their pickins'. Perhaps they, too, can leave this earth and you'll get to be their copilot.

256. WHO KNOWS WHY?

You have to come in and eat now.

"Why?"

It doesn't matter if Kenny's allowed to do that.

"Why?"

This piece doesn't fit in that slot.

"Why?"

You can't jump on the bed.

"Why?"

I'm going to get home late tonight.

"Why?"

"Why?" The question is short, sweet and often poignant. Take time to consider the array of possible answers rather than resort to the old, "Because I said so." Ask your child why *they* think the reason might be. Perhaps you'll understand that endless question better when you try to follow the logic of their answer. Hey, you can always resort to the classic oldie. Just remember that one day you won't be there to deliver the ultimate power play and they'd better have learned how to figure out the "why of it" for themselves.

257. THE GOOD FATHER

(Provided by Larry Turner)

> *Learn to enjoy your children's individuality as well as*
> *their diversity. Sometimes it's not until we look back*
> *that we suddenly capture the full meaning of the*
> *present. Take a look at my friend Larry, from whom*
> *we learn that those "aha!" moments not only bring*
> *clarity, but can even help us grin at ourselves.*

My three sons, all in their 20s, were home four days at Christmas. Judge Bork, Lilith, Raymond Chandler, and Noriega T-shirts were debated by day and night as if in some Umberto Eco novel.

Then one day they picked up a football and ran out to the street. Not one of them could throw or catch worth anything. What kind of father was I, who never taught his boys football?

Then the memories came back and the guilt vanished. We did play football when they were kids: I even broke Scott's collarbone.

258. STRANGER DANGER

FEAR

We make our children feel unsafe by warning them that all strangers are evil. I've heard many parents telling their children they shouldn't even talk to police officers who do not know their personal family "password" or code.

How can we make our children believe that no one—not even a police officer—can be trusted to help them if they are lost or in distress? On more than one occasion I've heard parents tell their children that if they weren't cautious every moment or didn't stop misbehaving (a threat of punishment), that someone might snatch them away. And we wonder why our children don't sleep at night!

Who is the monster here? Is it the one in a 100,000 who might actually commit this crime? Or is it the one inside the walls who, through flames of imagined horror, breathes fear into the babes, robbing them of their security and joy?

259. TOWER TIME

(Provided by Charleen Oligmueller)

Whatever your child's version of a tower,
it's worth the "climb."

Last summer, my two boys (then 2- and almost 4-years-old respectively) and I started having their morning snack in the tower of their playset in our backyard. Mom looked (and felt) a little silly crawling up there with them, but it turned out to be a lot of fun— for me and for them. We ate our snacks, laid on our backs, and looked at the clouds and the treetops, and told stories. This turned out to be the best part of all.

We took turns making up stories. The boys' stories started out quite simple and were often the same, but over time, the stories grew more complex. This activity has really helped them to develop their imaginations. And, on weekends or vacation days, Daddy has even been known to join us in the tower!

260. HAVING YOUR WAY...OR NOT

During a visit to our oldest son's, he had a major project for which he needed assistance. My husband offered to help. Within the first few minutes, it became obvious they didn't have the same notion as to how the task could best be completed. My husband, being a thoughtful engineer (and having tested my patience many times) felt things needed to go methodically. My son, being an active doer like myself, thought things needed to get done—*now!*

Much to my husband's credit, he backed away, zipped his lip, and allowed our adult son to go at his own pace, stepping in when asked rather than getting in a conflict. After all, every child has a right to his own way, whether it is ours or not.

261. RINGING IN A NEW YEAR

Isn't it wonderful when we each have a chance to believe every year, at least for a moment, that nothing but pure potential brings strong possibilities? Aside from the fallout and remnants of the last year, that boogery thing is behind us. *This* year we can conquer potty training, spelling lessons, driving school—the list goes on.

Guess what? Every day has a new year in front of it and an old one left behind. When a family member has been through a rough time, break out the goofy hats, rip up some paper (recycled, of course), procure a bottle of sparkling grape juice, and celebrate like it's the beginning of the new year that it is.

262. EXPLANATIONS OF LOVE

(Provided by Michael Lewis)

> *Sometimes we have to lower the boom. The balm that reconnects us afterwards, however, is lowering the voice with meaningful explanations.*

※※◎※※

After you scold your child, be sure to explain why you scolded. "Sammy, I'm sorry I yelled at you, but Daddy just wants you to know how dangerous it is to open the car door while we're moving. Daddy loves you more than anything and wants you to be safe. Okay?"

263. THREADS OF TIME

When I ask fathers how they remember feeling connected with their dads, playing catch is one of the assured responses. Simple throw and catch. Throw and catch. Throw and catch, like a thread weaving between them, tying them together. Mother and son, daddy and daughter, any combination you create. Throw and catch. Throw and catch. Each stitch strengthens the seam.

264. HONOR ONE ANOTHER

(Provided by Kimberly Warner)

Well before dawn on a snowy Christmas morning in 1961, I came into the world as the firstborn of ultimately four children of Gerry and Rosemary Welch. From the time I was old enough to tell when my birthday was, whenever anyone hears that date, their responses echo the same theme. "You poor thing, always shorted a present, what a rotten trick, bummer." And yet, that was never the case!

My parents are special, and they made sure my birthday was a day special for me. After Midnight Mass on Christmas Eve, we would return home knowing that Santa had come—finally falling asleep grasping our treasure for that year. Christmas day was spent visiting with relatives or just staying home, but that evening was always my birthday dinner. A birthday child in our house always got to pick the meal, so for us, the traditional Christmas dinner became my Mom's Famous Lasagna (we thought it worthy of fame)! After the meal my Mom would bring in the cake, then to the presents! No, I was never shorted, never made to feel anything but special on my birthday; my parents saw to that.

For 37 years that tradition never really varied, until this Christmas. We lost my Dad this past May and changed the traditions so as to get through the holidays. But I will always know how he and

Mom showed their love and care for me, in the way they took care of all—making me feel special.

265. SIMPLE PLEASURES

When I ask parents of wee ones when they feel most connected with their babies, they often answer it's when the baby smiles at them. There is an involuntary heart warming in the brightness of a happy response to our presence. And vice versa.

Presence. It's just flat out hard to replace.

266. CIRCLE OF LOVE

I went to England by myself for my 50th birthday. I spent the entire three weeks driving my hire car (commonly known as a rental in the United States) from here to there, mostly wandering Yorkshire, drinking in all the sites which for decades had beckoned me to come, come see. George and the boys cheered me on as I packed and planned.

In order to keep in touch and because something inside me compels me to write, I traveled with my laptop computer. Nearly everyday I would write a travel log detailing my discoveries, awe-inspired moments in the Dales (and screams of terror behind the wheel). I'd e-mail the messages to my sons and an accumulated list of others. At that time George didn't know how to use a computer so one of the boys would print out my e-mail and fax it to my home office where George would find it when he returned home from work. George relayed messages to the boys who added his sentiments into their news, updates, and responses to my great adventure.

No matter what anyone's age or location, with a bit of work, connections can be maintained. Figure out the how of it.

267. WHAT BIG EYES YOU HAVE

There are two ways to go through life: Looking for what's right and looking for what's wrong. I am a firm believer in the notion that you find what you look for. If you look for what's right in the world and the people who inhabit it, life will be brighter for both (all) of you. If a stranger demonstrates kindness or patience, has a lovely hair color, a stunning smile, a polite response, mesmerizing earrings, or a radio voice—tell them. Make their day; watch them brighten, too.

Your child is watching how you welcome, receive, and appreciate life (or not). Their attitude will be much shaped by yours. Teach them to look for what's right and they, too, will find it. Remember, part of what they're looking at is you.

268. GO TO IT!

(Provided by Sandy Koropp)

> *Believe in your children. To your core, to their faces, to the world, believe in your children.*

My grampa came to my dad's much-awaited career conference during his senior year in high school. (Okay, this was like 1955 and things were less focused then). A little background: my grampa had literally hidden under blankets crossing the Czech mountains in an ox-cart and sailed into Ellis Island. Grampa was then a Pennsylvania coal miner with his American-born brothers until he decided that he wanted an "office job" and came to Chicago. Several family members who stayed in Pennsylvania died of lung disease.

When my dad's high school counselor told them that my dad had a "solid B" but was not "college material," my grampa told him to "go to hell." He turned to my dad and said, "Son, you wanna go-ta college? You can do whateva you want. Dohn listen to this. You wanna go-ta college? You can go-ta college."

And my dad did. He went to college at Northwestern University and to their medical school. But more than any moment there, he defined himself by that moment in his high school counselor's office when his dad said "Go to Hell" to someone trying to define his spirit and his future for him. His dad didn't ponder the fancy frames of the counselor's educational degrees. His dad formed his son's soul for him that day. And though there were many complex moments yet to come in their relationship, it is that moment that lives on in our family's shared soul.

269. For better or for worse

One year George and I decided to go to New Orleans on a vacation. As is sometimes the case with we opposites who attract, I couldn't get enough of the food, music, ethnic diversity, and "earthiness." It all couldn't be too loud, late, or delicious. With George, the surroundings can be *all* of those things, rather quickly. Although we had a fabulous time in spite of our differences, (I was born to wallow in that place) I thought several times about how fun it would also be to one day be there with Bret, our oldest son. Now there's a guy who would "do" New Orleans the way his mom would. This I knew. And so mother and son made a commitment to do just that one day.

It wasn't long before the opportunity opened up. I received an invitation for a speaking engagement nearby the New Orleans area. I phoned Bret, gave him the dates I'd be there, and made arrangements for him to join me afterwards for a good and rowdy mother and son time. The evening of our meeting, Bret arrived at the hotel room at 11:45 p.m. after taking a shuttle from the airport. In order to save money for our adventure, we were sharing a room with two double beds. We were both tired, chatted a few minutes, and decided to crash. Quickly we were sound asleep. And then the phone rang. It was my husband.

"Is Bret there?" he asked, with a strange tone in his voice. "Yes," I answered. My husband had the horrid duty to announce that my father had died. Although George had known about this for a couple hours, he waited until he knew I'd be in the company of my son to deliver the shocking news.

All the moments we share with our children are not ones of joy. But I can assure you of this, even the deep wounds of death can create abiding moments of tender connection.

270. Dot to dot

The inborn, human urge to connect certainly expands farther than parent and child. In our suburban communities, the last few years I've noticed a definite trend toward evidence of that need via the immense emergence of sidewalk cafes, bagel places, and community coffee shops with outdoor seating. The popularity of the big old front porch has returned, making us visible one to another rather than locked away in our oh-so-private backyards. After a couple decades of "It's all about me," I believe we're lonesome for one another. We need to be strung together, if only for Saturday morning sits, Sunday afternoon sandwiches at the local hangout— where, like Cheers, everybody knows our name—or evenings when we watch the world go by from our porch swing.

Discuss how important a sense of community is with your child. Wave to people you know, and those you don't. Invite others to come sit a spell with you guys; accept invitations to do the same. When we are all strung together, we create a web of security in our neighborhoods; one that can be felt by everyone.

271. Get the message

Once upon a single-mothering time I had a very bad mothering day. (Okay, I had many of them.) I was late, yet again, picking up my son from daycare. The guilt-plagued, last mom to arrive, my tired self, and the sorrowful look on my son's tiny face crushed my heart. Tired, tired, tired. I'm sure any working parent can relate to this scenario.

Picture this: You leave work when you should and arrive to daycare on time. Your child, even though he or she may have a tired, tiny face, isn't delivered the nonverbal message that he or she is on the bottom of your priority list. No matter how you explain how important everything was you had to do that made you late, they receive one message: "It was all more important than you, child of mine. You're the one thing that could be moved to the bottom of my list." And there is no other way for that to be interpreted because it's true.

If you're not the one who does the picking up but you're the one getting home to your family late every evening, the message you deliver is still the same. If you're the one who is home all day with the kids and all they hear is "later," it is still the same.

Do something about it. Not only will your child be honored, but you'll alleviate yourself from a burden: Guilt is a heavy load to carry around. I know. I've carried it.

272. AFTER WORDS

(Provided by Michael Lewis)

After you read your child a story, hand them the book and encourage them to tell you about it. You'll be amazed at how much they remember, and how creative and imaginative your little one can be.

273. NOT LIKE ME

What comes naturally to one isn't what necessarily comes naturally to another. How do we bridge the gap of differences between us and our kids, while also feeding and cultivating their individuality? One of the ways is to watch the child, then watch for opportunities that fit their developing individuality.

A friend of mine has a beautiful daughter who is interested in many things my friend isn't. Her daughter enjoys crafts; Mom discovered their church has a ladies' sewing circle. Although no youth were involved at that time, the ladies were happy to embrace her daughter into their group. Not only is the child's talent for needlework fed, but the circle of people who care about her has grown, as well.

274. ROLE MODEL

I was waiting in my car on our side street to make a left onto the main street near my house. I realized I had an opening if I moved swiftly and stayed to the inside lane as I crossed oncoming traffic. (It was a very busy time of day on the road.) When I gunned the car, my glasses and a wad of papers on the dashboard began to skid. Stretching my full length to keep them from skidding out the open window on the passenger side, I jerked the car a bit. Now mind you, I didn't veer into the other lane; but for a split second, I looked like I might. I suspected I caused the oncoming driver's heart to skip a beat.

I looked in my rearview mirror and saw her approaching me on the passenger side and pushed the electronic button to roll that window down, preparing to apologize. As she pulled up beside me I opened my mouth to speak and she began screaming a string of obscenities at me. "You *blanken blank*! I have my *blanken* kids in the car! What were you *blanken* thinkin'? What a *blanken blank*! Can't you see I have my *blanken* kids in my car?!"

Okay, to call me a "*blanken blank*" was one thing. But to do it not only in front of her kids but then to refer to them as the same *blanken* was stunning. All I could think to say, in a relatively quiet tone of voice, was, "Yes, I see you have your kids in the car and you're not being a very good example right now, are you?" Up rolled my window; there was no use trying to talk to her. She continued to scream and added visual hand signals to her production.

Which was worse? Her heart skipping a beat, or her children learning that this is how you respond to a careless moment. (And that they, too, were referred to as *blanken blanks*?)

Listen to yourself when you speak. Would you like someone talking to or about you that way?

275. PERIODS OF ADJUSTMENT

The first time Brian returned home for a visit after he'd gone off to college was an exciting time for the Baumbichs. Brian's sad and empty shrine of a room sat unoccupied, awaiting his messy, yet lively, occupancy. George and I looked forward to lots of meaningful time together after our baby's three-month absence. I cooked. I cleaned. George helped. We cleared our calendar. We prepared so as to have nothing to do but be fully present to him.

Surprise: He wasn't around much. We heard the door slam when he left to visit every friend he'd ever made his entire life and bang open when he returned, asking what was for dinner. I found myself slipping into rather juvenile poutiness over feelings of rejection. Talk about my long-suffering, parental connectedness being kicked aside! (Okay, I know this is dramatic but it's how I felt!)

By the time he returned to school I had learned a valuable lesson. I wasn't sure what it was, but I knew I'd learned something because darn it if I hadn't at least learned something, well...what was the point in having kids to start with? But seriously, what I learned while crying and weeping to friends about my nasty little child who abandoned me (okay, I wasn't quite over it yet) was that his behavior was normal and it didn't mean he didn't love us. I was prepared for this the next time he came home, happily accepting whatever was there to receive. And to help me prepare for that, during a sudden and truly inspirational vision, I joyfully turned his shrine of a room into a guest retreat!

276. AHA!

I was watching television one night and a gentleman unrecognized by me made the following statement: "If you are a parent, you have to give your kids the opportunity to not be you." How true.

277. HANG TOUGH

When I hopped in a limousine this morning on my way to the airport, I was thrilled to be greeted by an acquaintance I hadn't seen for years. We'd belonged to a Bible study together and our sharing and prayers over pressing and often intimate details became a welcome weekly ritual during that course in our lives.

"How's your son?" I inquired, knowing she would know which one I was talking about. Much prayer had been sent heaven-bound on his behalf.

"You won't believe it," she exclaimed. "He's a junior in high school now and he's taking honors chemistry!" We did everything but hug, which I'm sure we would have had it not been for the fact we were seat belted into our side-by-side positions.

"Oh that's wonderful!" I shouted. "What a great triumph and hope for parents," I went on to say, "to have heard you tell about all the concerns and trials you went through and to now learn that he's doing so well!"

No matter what your religious persuasion, share your prayers. They connect us *all* to those for whom we pray.

278. BUILDING PROJECT

I talked to a gentleman who had recently lost his dad. When I asked about how they connected, at first he indicated—both verbally and through the pained look on his face—that this was a bad topic. Their relationship during his growing years had been fraught with humiliation, ridicule, and his inability to live up to his dad's expectations.

In recent years, however, there was an occasion that brought them together. His father stayed at his home for three weeks to help with a major remodeling project. It was during that side-by-side working time, he said, that a few corners were smoothed, both in the project and in their relationship.

Side-by-side time working together. Patching. Reshaping. Building.

279. BUILDING PROJECT, TAKE 2

Three-time dad Bernie Ruser has a heart for those seeking to start over. He volunteered to go with a work crew to pull wire on a house being built as a Habitat for Humanity project. He decided to take his 5-year-old son Jeffrey with him. Jane, Bernie's wife, told me about it in an e-mail.

"They filled their tool belts the night before with all the essential tools. Jeffrey could not stop showing people his belt—he was so proud of it. He was so funny. They had a blast and came home very dirty. But the best part was seeing Bernie carry him through the front door at 10:30 p.m. sound asleep with his tool belt still on! Precious!"

Side-by-side time working together; building relationships.

280. SAYING YES

(Provided by Dave and Cathy Garland)

During the frenzy of the holidays, our 9-year-old son reminded us what Christmas and family time is really all about. In an essay titled "Memories are Gifts," Ben wrote the following:

"Dad, I remember the time when you were working down in the back of the gloomy laundry room. You were working so hard. I bet your arms started to hurt. I was watching TV and I really wanted to play some basketball. You were in there shaving that door. Then, I came in and said, 'Dad, do you want to play basketball?' When you said, 'Yes,' I was filled with joy.

"That time was very special for me. I think you did a nice job on those doors. Actually, you did a very good job. Better yet, you did an awesome job. But you did an even better job playing with me. Thank you for making this memory stick with me. Love, Ben."

Ben gave this essay as a Christmas present. It is handwritten and covered with simple red construction paper. It's perfect and couldn't be any nicer because of what it represents. To us and hopefully to all of you, memories are true gifts.

281. ABSENCE

In a recent national report it was stated by one authority that there is a widespread belief that "young people aren't getting the parenting they need because of parents who are emotionally absent from the home." Read that last sentence again. Not just absent, but present and *emotionally* absent.

The upshot and consequences of this according to the article: "teen drug use, violence and sexual activity all converge to a broader concern about a large minority of children growing up without a sense of right and wrong, respect for authority, or a sense of responsibility." Are you there emotionally?

282. ADMIRATION

Webster's New World Dictionary, Second College Edition, defines the word "admire" this way: "to regard with wonder, delight, and pleased approval." To tell your child you know they are talented is good. To say you've noticed their (*fill in the blank*) is good. To say you're impressed is good. To say you regard *anything* about them with wonder, delight, and approval would float just about anybody's boat and keep it motoring for quite a long time. (You can even write and tell *me* that any day! I promise I'll be genuinely very excited and I'll thank you profusely.)

283. LET THEM IN

(Provided by Gundega Korsts)

Connect with your children by letting them *into* your heart. Give in to that feeling that you are more than one person: that your children are part of you. This doesn't mean owning them, or being less than complete when they are gone. It means that, wherever they are and whatever they are doing, whatever the triumphs or the crises, they are with you, because they are in your heart. And you are with them, because when the connection of love is real, they feel it, too.

I learned this when my daughter and her husband were living an ocean and a continent away. I hadn't seen them in more than a year. When a friend commiserated with me, saying how hard it must be to have my children so far away, I replied, without a thought, "But they're not far away. They're right *here*." (With a thump on my chest at the "here.") That connection is part of what carried me through the grieving after my daughter died later that same year, when "the last time I saw her" turned out to be the last time ever indeed. But she had never been far.

284. Hard lessons

I can only remember overtly, out-and-out, and repeatedly defying my parents on one issue in my entire growing-up years: The time that they dictated I could no longer see a very special friend. There was no talk about this beforehand. No explanations. No input, rebuttal, or allowance for evidence to the contrary that I might have to ward off or dispel whatever was bugging them. The friend came to pick me up for a scheduled pickup. Mom met the friend at the door and told him never to see me again. When I arrived in the kitchen, that was that. I was told the same thing: We were not to see each other ever again.

Although my parents did an excellent job of rearing me—and I do mean excellent—this was one big mistake that forced me to disobey them (at least that's the way I saw it in my 16-year-old eyes). The action on my part was rooted in the unfairness of it all. It wasn't just that they didn't *want* me to see him again, but that whatever their case was, it was not presented to me. Guilty without trial or jury or talk—and perhaps most importantly, completely contrary to the spirit by which I'd been raised: To never judge by opinions or appearances. And so I, witnessing nothing evil or disrespectful about him or how he'd treated me (and in order to show my trust in his trust) snuck around seeing him. Several times they found out, and accusals, arguing, and reprimands broke out. Always, my argument was the same: Whatever you think he is or isn't, he's never evidenced it with me!

Eventually my parents acquiesced (having no obvious control over this anyway) and allowed me to see him. Eventually life ran its natural course and we "broke up," which might have even happened sooner had we not been "hurled together" against the "foe." Who knows.

If you disapprove of your child's friends (and there can be times this is wisdom), talk to them about it. Ask them what they like about the friend. Be respectful and truly listen. Share your concerns and see how they answer. Just be careful about lowering an unfair boom; it might spring back and whap you one. Better to distract than destroy.

285. SWITCHAROONI

I remember when Brian went through about a year-long period where he screamed about his socks. They touched his toes, his toes pulled on them, the socks pinched them, or something else. He would take his socks on and off, throwing fits in between, screaming and yelling at his socks as he attempted to get them on just so. At one point I finally popped the budget and bought the more expensive socks that didn't have a seam on the end of the toe, hoping this would help. Although it didn't end the problem, it did help us get through that year of "Sockitis" which just about drove us all to that great padded place in the Chop Buster's Hall of Fame. He finally outgrew whatever it was and was pleased we had at least attempted, through new socks, to kill the "Evil Sock Monsters of Torment."

I tell you this because sometimes concessions, as irrational as they may be—such as spending extra money on the sock budget when you don't *really* need to buy socks—is a wise parenting move in order to maintain not only connections, but sanity. In the grand scheme of things, socks just aren't worth going to the mat for.

286. *THELMA AND LOUISE*

(Provided by Donna O'Brien)

Every year, my younger daughter and I go on what has come to be called our "Thelma and Louise" trip. Although (happily) it doesn't end quite so dramatically as the movie for which it was named, this trip for just the two of us has proven again and again to be a source of memories and stories for the rest of the year, hopefully longer.

Together we have eaten chocolates in Hershey, Pennsylvania, rode "Batman, The Ride" (where I was the only one older than 22 in line!), traversed Door County by bike, and checked out the various delights in the Dells of Wisconsin. The latter included the gray-hair inducing experience of watching my youngest child bungee-jump into the stratosphere (an event I don't recommend to the faint-hearted).

What I do recommend is taking the time to be alone with each child. Never underestimate the incredible impact of alone time in a car. Something about sitting side-by-side while miles go by that induces real conversation.

This annual road trip has created for my daughter and I a unique opportunity to get to know one another without any of the other distractions of family and daily life.

287. If only...

George and I were strolling down the boardwalk, enjoying a vacation moment along the shores of Deluth, Minnesota, when two moms pushing strollers, toddler in each, appeared over the hill, sauntering down the boardwalk. Their older sons, probably about 4 years old, were jumping from giant boulder to giant boulder closer to the water. One of the boys hollered "Follow me!" while motioning a giant "come-this-a-way" wave. It became clear he was used to leading and his small army-of-one loved following.

"Okay boys, it's time to go," the ring leader's mom yelled. "Not now!" oh cap-i-tan replied. "Yes now!" Mom responded, a perky lilt in her voice. Ever farther into battle and away from the moms the two fearless voyagers traveled, completely ignoring the other voice.

"Bradley! *Now!*" Mom finally yelped in her "Biggest Mommy Voice." The troops, now paying no heed whatsoever to the other voice, continued their exploration to far-away lands. After a couple more unanswered blasts, Mom began screaming her obvious and familiar last warning countdown: "One! Two!" She hesitated about a half count after two when the captain whirled on his heels and seized the opening to scream at his mom, "You're fired!"

Mom's mouth flew open and then it registered what she'd been told. An odd smile spread across her face. I heard her mumble something like, "Good!" as she spun the baby carriage and disappeared back over the hill from which they'd first appeared, her friend close behind. (Obviously leadership runs in families.) Of course the captain and his troop eventually came screaming after them.

And now for the moral of this story: Even when your kids fire you and you joyfully and cheerfully accept their dictum, they will undoubtedly find you and change their minds. But accept it anyway, if only for one bliss-filled moment.

288. MODERN-DAY STORYTELLING

(Provided by Marty Dome)

Keep an ongoing e-mail conversation with your college kids. Write to them at least once a week if only to say: "You are wonderful and I love you lots and lots and the cat sends along a big kiss." Print out their message to you.

I have done this for both of my children and when they are finished with college I will put these messages into a book for each of them. It will be a wonderful diary for them to remember that freshman year roommate who was impossible to get along with, that terrible organic chemistry class they struggled through, that awesome play they were in, that boy/girl friend that at the time was so wonderful, or what fun we all had at parent's weekend.

Don't tell them about this, of course, so they won't be intimidated about writing their messages, so they can be blessed by the surprise.

289 ANIMAL LIFE

While browsing in a store that sold lots of fluffy stuff, I ran across a sign that read, "Raising a child is like being pecked to death by a chicken." Ain't it the truth?! How many times have you said:

"Don't ask me again!"

"How many times do I have to tell you....?"

"What did I say about your clean shirt?"

"Do you want another time-out?"

So why might your child be pecking, pecking, and pecking? Read those questions through again. And again. Was your head or finger bobbing and wagging? As though *you* were pecking?

Oh, life in the barnyard. Ouch.

290. ALL DRIED UP

A mom told me about the time her child came toward her, wet thumb raised in the air, just having extracted it from his mouth. "Mom," he said, looking forlorn and lost, "my thumb ran out of juice."

There are days when adults feel exactly like that. Sharing that information with our child is an honest thing to do. You'd be amazed how understanding and comforting they can be sometimes.

291. LITERARY MILES

TRAVEL

(Provided by Will Kilkeary)

One of the places that my daughter and I connect best is in the car. We are forced to take long car rides often, which gives us both a captive audience (as long as we don't turn on the radio). We have a number of ways that we interrelate during these trips, after we have shared what is new or interesting in our lives. One is through audio books.

I choose a book that is equal to, or slightly ahead of, my daughters reading ability and listen to it myself to make sure that it has some literary value beyond just a story. My daughter and I then listen to it in the car. At the end of each side of the tape, we discuss what we think will happen. We talk about any hints (foreshadowing) that we have noticed—both those that have happened and those that we think might happen. We talk about how the characters are growing or changing in the book. We talk about symbols.

As a result of this interaction: My daughter enjoys reading more, readily discusses the merits (or lack there of) of everything she reads, and seems to be more comfortable talking about things in general. I also get my reading ability sharpened, get to hear some great stories, and get many things pointed out to me that I have missed.

292. Interesting perceptions

At age 54, I find I haven't been in sync with my surrounding culture. I'm currently experiencing a minor "hippie phase" which I missed the first time around. This is perhaps best seen by the bead curtain stringing across my office door and my fascination with even danglier earrings than I've always worn (if that is humanly possible).

I was talking to Bret long-distance one day and announced to him that I was—though very mildly, yet nonetheless happily—participating in my hippie phase which I'd missed during the 1960s. He was surprised, "Mom! I was the only kid in third grade who had sprouts on my sandwiches!"

"And that made me a hippie?" I asked incredulously. "Good grief Bret! Don't you remember we grew them for a Cub Scout project?" (I was an ace Den Mother!) Somehow that served to him as even more proof for his point of view.

Ask your any-aged children how they would describe you to others. (I'd suggest fastening your seatbelt first.)

293. Terrible twos

I was doing a radio interview after *Don't Miss Your Kids!* was released and a caller wanted me to dispel the myth of the "Terrible Twos." I was quiet for a second and then I could do nothing but speak the truth: "Truly, I don't remember them being so hot! In fact, I remember thinking, 'So this is where the phrase came from!'"

In order to help survive that phase (and not to be discouraging but it can last up to three years), make sure you take a lot of time to study your sleeping child. Plant the image in your brain. When they're running around holding their backsides and simply won't potty train, you will remember what they looked (and smelled) like before the nightmare, screaming, throwing fits, "dumpster in the panster" phase.

294. Eager Anticipation

I was attending a high-profile, high-priority business conference in Chicago. When we were dismissed for lunch, the crunch was on to find our way to restaurants, slam down some food, and get back to the conference in time for our first five-minute appointment with a big deal editor. Miss a minute, lose a minute.

As I began my charge across the street, pedestrian traffic came to a sudden standstill. Clearly the little man on the walk/don't walk sign was walking—why weren't we? Just when I was at the edge of elbowing people out of my way or at the very least bellowing like a cow giving birth, I saw the obstruction. A kneeling father, one small child under each arm, was perched right at the edge of the curb. They were each staring straight up, as was the growing ensemble.

"Keep watching," he instructed. "Here it comes! Get ready!" I could do nothing but join in this mass of bodies, staring at the digital clock hanging off the corner of the bank. And when the next minute clicked on, we all cheered.

Miss a minute. Lose a minute. Seize a minute. With or without your kids. The choice is yours.

295. Held Captive

"Mom, I'm home!" I'd shout when I walked through the back porch door.

"I'm down here ironing, honey!" I'd hear from the basement. I'd bound down the steps, bust through the door, and plop myself down near Mom. She'd be grinning from ear to ear when she saw me and then she'd ask me about my day. I'd hurl myself here and there, dramatically rendering the highs and lows. Sometimes I'd launch into one of my many impersonations because it tickled her so and I delighted in her laughing responses to my efforts. I can still hear the steam from the iron hissing as she'd set the iron upright to rearrange the fabric or take a big drink of her sweating, home-brewed iced tea. Mom was a captive audience behind that ironing board.

Not many of our clothes today need pressing and to that I say, hip hip hurray! And yet...all the running around is just too much. We drop shirts off at the dry cleaners. We drop recycling at the curb and we drop our kids off for lessons and sports and club activities. Days of the grace of a captive audience have seemingly been dropped off someplace, too.

Mom and/or Dad, vow to plant yourself and be caught captive. Vow to plant yourself.

296. SECOND GUESSES

"Mom, what does bad hamburger really smell like?" This is not the question you want to hear on the other end of a phone line when your first born child is hundreds of miles away.

"Honey, if you have to ask—if you feel like there's reason enough to call long distance and ask—I'd say throw it away."

Don't spend so much time longing for the day when a child's endless questions finally stop that you wish away the blissful possibility for a moment like this.

297. THE NIGHT THE LIGHTS DIDN'T GO OUT

Sometimes what doesn't happen is as important as what does. The main thing is that we prepare for it together.

(This correspondence came to me in an e-mail from Bonnie Epperson, dated January 1, 2000.)

Well, It's 12:35 a.m.! My computer is working and electricity is on. My bottled water will be drunk or poured down the drain, and all the stored can goods will eventually be gobbled up. The anticipation that last second before midnight was somewhat of a disappointment. The kids all wanted the lights to go out so we could live like *Little House on the Prairie*. You know, cooking over the fire in the fireplace, all living in one room just to stay warm, etc. It's all over. The little ones just said, "Is that all?!"

No, child, the memories have yet to ripen.

298. SHARING A LOSS

DEATH

A grieving friend asked, "How do we explain death to kids?" I responded, "How can we explain it to ourselves when our hearts feel wrenched from our bodies?"

"I would think you'd almost want to celebrate the deceased person's life and relive happy memories of Grandpa, a favorite pet, whatever or whomever—through photos, testifying at their grave site, or whatever," he said. "Yes. Of course," I said. "But we also want to be real. How do we explain? We grieve. We ask. We weep. We celebrate life. We weep again for what is no longer with us or never got a chance to flower. We allow our children to witness each of our phases of grief so they can be free to do the same, and we hold them close when we laugh again. And cry again. And laugh again."

299. WHERE IN THE WORLD IS...

If your family is spread out all over the country, with one set of grandparents here, and another there, and Aunt Sarah *way* over there, get a map of the United States (or world, if need be), plop it down on the kitchen table, rally the troops, and spend a leisurely half hour or so with your kids pointing out where all those people live. Talk about them. Explain how they're related. See who can remember the last time you saw them. Rather than your children feeling a bit isolated from extended family, perhaps it will help them to learn that you are all surrounded by—and therefore connect to—a bigger circle of love than they imagined.

300. RAINBOW CONNECTION

(Provided by Denise Beverly)

> *Notice how this connection began with the statement, "I struggled to be close with her." That is an action sentence.*

❧❦❧

I have four children: a 10 1/2-year-old daughter, 8-year-old twins (son and daughter), and a 5-year-old daughter. I have been looking at each of my children as they grow to see what connection I can have with them besides just being their mom. I was having trouble with my 8-year old daughter. Her personality is very different from mine and I struggled to be close with her.

Then our elementary school had a special night of art. They invited the parents to go with their child to this event. Sarah and I signed up. We had a great time. The theme was "watercolors." The art teacher asked us to think about a place we enjoy and to draw it together. We came up with the idea of snow capped mountains reflecting in a lake. I drew the outline of the picture and together we added color. It was so pretty when we were done.

Sarah loves to draw and I enjoy crafts too. So we connected like we never have before. It was such a nice evening. The picture was signed, "made by Sarah and Mom" and hangs proudly in her bedroom. We came home and got out our watercolors and markers. The rest of the kids and I made more pictures that night and the following night. We even got books from the library to see works done by other artists.

Not only was this a one-on-one time with Sarah, but it stretched out to the other children as well.

301. THE REST OF THE STORY

I recently spent a great deal of time, energy, and words composing an e-mail expressing my sense of rejection over a particular event. Poor me, I bemoaned in an oh-so-appropriate choice of words. Mean you, I accused, in an even more carefully selected yet decisive set of words.

And then came a surprising response that clarified that not only had the accused person not perpetrated the small crime they'd been accused of, but that they were also a victim, unable to keep from passing along a piece of their misery and in fact up to their gills with struggling to hang on as well. Ouch.

The same is true for our children. Might there be more to their story than meets our spying eye? Perhaps we should ask before jumping to conclusions and spilling our parental guts and punishments.

302. CENTER OF ATTENTION

I was raised on a small farm and I loved creating centerpieces for our table. I'd gather wild flowers and sometimes bits of hay and put plastic horses in them, like a barnyard scene. Other times I'd use my jewelry to create some exotic concoction. When I became a mom, I occasionally challenged one of my sons to decorate the table. Hot Wheels, pretty rocks...who knew what might become our focal point?

The decoration itself wasn't ever what really mattered. However, the fact that my mom asked me to be creative (and gave me no boundaries) was the real prize. And my boys loved that one of their favorite things would become the center of attention for an evening, and thereby so did they.

Try it. You might like it. You might find that a few Barbies, some stacked up Hot Wheels, or a robot who can transform into a rocket or a monster, will make even the fastest of fast foods seem more festive. Your teens can participate too! It's a good, nonthreatening way to find out what they might hold in esteem.

303. ARTISTIC EXPRESSIONS

I called to talk to a friend today who happened to have a house full of kids: her own three and several of her kids' friends. They were all laughing and carrying on in the background, busy drawing all over themselves with body paints, she said.

"What fun!" I bellowed. "Why don't you paint yourself a tattoo on each ankle?" She thought she just might do that. And then it struck me: have a "Family Paints The Family Night." Now that ought to produce a few raucous Kodak moments!

304. SHARE YOUR MUSIC

(Provided by Heidi Snopko)

Children learn about music in school and church. Many take music lessons. They all have favorite artists on MTV and the radio. Use this interest in music and song to connect with your kids by sharing your music with them. It not only reinforces the music skills they learn in school, but shows them that you are a human creature as well, with interests and pleasures and (well, maybe) good taste. And it helps pass down the history of your family.

I sing my children to sleep using the lullabies and hymns that my mother used to sing to me and my brother, in both English and German (my mother's native language). It is truly touching when a child asks her tone-deaf Mommy (that'd be me!) to sing "that song Uncle Phil used to like."

I also share my favorite popular music with my kids, both by listening to current favorites in the car and singing along (loudly!), and by listening to recordings of older music that I loved when I was younger. I smile when they turn on the radio and say "Mommy! Here's your favorite song!" And I nearly swooned this Thanksgiving when my 4-year-old crawled up into my lap after dinner, singing the Joni Mitchell hit, "Big Yellow Taxi": "Dey pave pa'adise, put up a pahkin laht."

305. FINGERPRINTS OF TIME

I still have a few Golden Books from my childhood. They are torn—some with missing covers. And for the most part, they are all scribbled up with crayons. It was obvious this once-upon-a-time girl loved "reading" from those battle-worn beauties way before she actually recognized any of the words. I could sense the tone in my adult voice melting a bit at first sight of those colorful and familiar words and illustrations when the boys and I pulled them out of a dusty box. I said, "Ohhhhh! I remember *this* one!" I grinned at the site of my printed name, shaky with youth's first attempts as I stated my name atop all the scribbles. Deep within myself, I heard the sound of my mother's voice as she read them to me, felt her arms brushing against mine as she turned the pages, as I sat curled on her lap. I remembered her listening to my halting renditions.

Allow your children to play with their books and toys. Really play. All those collectible things will one day eventually fade away. Nothing stays new forever, no matter how we coddle and protect it. Sure, they might bring a pretty penny one day if they are un-opened, tags on, no dust, in their original boxes. But what memories will they hold? May the wear and tear become part of your connection as years of fingerprints overlap, one generation to the next.

306. The long haul

Travel

We decided to take the "extended driving vacation" the summer before Bret entered high school. We figured the trip should be during that summer, because sports, jobs, and girls might undoubtedly soon crimp our abilities to be gone for two or more weeks at a time. Because we were Midwesterners (and because we were dumb), we decided to take on the entire West: Black Hills, Mt. Rushmore, Yellowstone, Boise, Disneyland... oh boy didn't we have fun? (Well, *most* of the time. Some moments— okay days—were completely torturous. Desert sun and flaring tempers from oh so much time together seemed to dehydrate all of our niceness.)

Before we left, someone told me we'd be sorry if we didn't keep a vacation journal. Although we'd never done such a thing before, I decided that on this long of a trip, memories would probably all run together if we didn't. That is a fact; by the second week we'd already forgotten some of what we did the first and were checking the journal just to give evidence to our "discussion" (*read:* war). That journal is a very funny (okay, most of the time) reminder of the great driving vacation. I'd suggest you try it, even for the short-haul trips. Have your kids make their own entries, drawing pictures, writing poetry, or just scribbling in their attempt to depict what they've seen. Marking time helps you pay more attention to it.

307. SACRED MOMENTS

When Brian was little, he would sit down by me and say, "Scratch my head," and I would. Sometimes he'd even put his head in my lap, and nearly falling to sleep as I fiddled with his hair, rubbed his scalp, and felt the familiar contour of his head. If he'd been a cat, I'm sure he would have been purring, he would become so relaxed.

As an adult, he still likes to have his head scratched, although opportunities are very few and far between. But I delight in these sacred moments to touch my baby aside from a hello or goodbye hug. I still rub his scalp, fiddle with his hair, and feel the familiar contour of his head, all which can be accomplished even as he sits in front of a computer monitor.

There is magic and God's grace in span-the-decades moments such as this between a child and parent. Hush now. Hush and find your own moments.

308. WHEN THE SHOE FITS

(Provided by Paul Halvey)

Sometimes we need to let the children direct our paths.

❦

Usually, it's the grown-ups struggling to get the toddler to focus on something long enough for it to sink in. But parents can have their brain spasms, too. Once, when trying to decide how to spend a free afternoon, I asked Bridget if she would like to go to the nearby park, the one with the big, bus-shaped climbing toy. Before she could answer, I suggested breaking out our crayons and coloring books. Or we could read. Or have a tea party. Or...

Bridget walked over to me, gently grabbed my shoulders, and turned me to face her. Then she moved her face mere inches from mine, and spoke slowly and deliberately, so I wouldn't miss a word. "I...want...to...go...to...the...park...and...drive...the...bus."

309. KEY WORD

There is a wise rabbinical maxim that goes something like this: "A man will have to give an account on the judgment day for every good thing which he might have enjoyed and did not."

Notice that this powerful wake-up statement says "enjoy." Not endure, sacrifice for, cultivate, discipline, read millions of child-rearing manuals to figure out, get into the best school, bake the best cookies for, or whatever. Enjoy. That is the key word for today. Certainly, our children are among the good things. Yes, enjoy.

310. MISSION: POSSIBLE

Write a family mission statement. Ask your kids what they believe your family stands for, or what they would like for it to. Let them be privy to the discussion between your spouse and yourself regarding this mutual goal. What sets your family apart from others? What matters to you as a family that is reflected in your behaviors and surroundings? What falls short?

If the life you're leading as a family doesn't line up with the mission statement, discuss what small or large steps can be taken to get them in sync. Discuss how accountability factors might be set in place to honor the commitment.

It's good to know where you're aimed and that you're all looking at the same shoreline.

311. SAY IT AGAIN

"Ten years from now it won't make a bit of difference, and maybe even tomorrow—if you let it." Pearls of wisdom from my dad. I've heard the "10 years" part of that from many mouths over my lifetime. But that last portion, the bit that gives us permission to let "it" go sooner and reminds us that we *can*, well that is pure Vic Brown. Pure inspiration and pure truth.

So often you hear people on television quoting their parents, as in, "My dad always used to say ...." Not the world or the guy next door, but my dad, my mom, the ones who raised us up, like my grannie used to say. The impact of repetition is amazing, especially when it's personalized, and out of the mouths of those whom we treasure...and believe.

312. FULL CIRCLE

(Provided by Sandy Schuler)

> *Sometimes one small connection leads to the next and before you know it, generations gather around a campfire.*

Back in the mid 1970s, my husband Bob and our son Bobby became members of Indian Guides. Appropriately, when asked what Indian names they would like to be known as, they chose Big Bobcat and, you guessed it, Little Bobcat. Over the next few years, Big Bobcat and Little Bobcat attended monthly meetings with other dads and their sons, spent hours with their heads together designing the sure-to-win model race car for the yearly Indian Guide "Indy 500" and of course, being Indian Scouts, every so often a camping experience occurred—once in a cave, complete with bats!

It was during these years when Big Bobcat came home from a monthly meeting and told me about a group from our area who was forming a once-a-month camping club. At the time, we had two other children besides Little Bobcat and never seemed to have the opportunity (or cash) to get away on a real vacation, staying in motels and eating three meals a day in restaurants. So we figured this would be a guaranteed (and not too expensive) way to get away once a month with the kids. The decision to do this, even though we had to learn a lot about camping, proved to be a positive experience beyond our expectations. We were fortunate to involve ourselves with a group where both the adults and the children clicked. Throughout all these years, all our children have continued to love camping, including the two more who came along by the mid-1980s.

Camping has been a great experience for all of us, but especially for Little Bobcat and his dad who are like two peas in a pod. Little

Bobcat is now a husband and dad; he has his own family, his own camper, and his own boat. We're proud of our Little Bobcat. And when we pull into the campsite next to the one occupied by *our* Little Bobcat, Big Bobcat and me find our connections coming full circle when our Little Bobcat's son Bobby—now the Littlest Bobcat—knocks on our camper door and says, "Grandpa, are you ready to go fishin?"

313. Wall of fame

I attended a luncheon in a home filled with antiques. From one room to the next, my eyes and senses reveled in the opportunity to step back into yesterday. This, of course, isn't counting the central air conditioning that kept us from melting, electric water cooler that delivered chilled-just-right quenching at the push of a button, the double-wide refrigerator freezer which harbored all the desserts...you get the picture. Yes, aside from those necessities (and I do mean that), all "furniture and fixins" had been collected from their own family estates, auctions, antique shops, and wherever else they ran across them. It felt cozy, reminded me of a simpler life, and was distinctive and tasteful. Even the artwork was comprised of the old sepia-tone photos of their ancestry. Everything was made up of quiet colors and just oozed with century-old fingerprints and stories.

And then we entered the family room, which was entirely decorated in bold, primary colors. Modern fabrics, over-stuffed furniture, comfy throws...But the most primary of colors was the artwork: It was entirely made up of their children's dated, matted and exquisitely framed finger paintings, drawings, and collages. Their children, who were now adults themselves. The entire home was a reminder of what mattered, then and now: family.

314. For real

No matter how silly or unimportant your child's latest traumatic experience might be, honor it with care and attention. Swallow the laugh if you have to; stifle the sigh or groan; nix the smarty retort. To hear the words, "Don't be silly," or "Just forget about it," in response to a real emotion is crushing, no matter how old you are.

315. WESTERN WISDOM

"Never kick a cow chip on a hot day," says Texas Bix Bender in his book titled *Don't Squat With Yer Spurs On! The Cowboy's Guide to Life.* To this, I would add: Don't take a kid shopping when they're already cranky. And don't ask them if you look stupid. And don't assume they know what to say when you ask them, in your most authoritative voice, "What do you say, Mister?" because you might be surprised and humiliated at the answer, especially if it's given in public. And don't leave any "parts" on a baby boy uncovered when you're changing his diaper. And don't ask a teenage girl if she'd like to know what you're thinking about her clothes. If you do any of these things, you might as well squat with yer spurs on and kick a cow chip on a hot day. Trust me on this one: Either would be more fun.

316. WORD BY WORD

I see television talk shows where family members have quit talking to one another over an incident. Years go by and the conflict spreads—even though some can no longer even remember how it all began. Generations of bloodlines and stories knit together by time and tradition, severed. Brothers and sisters, sisters and sisters, parent and child...the sturdiness of strength in relationships reduced to ashes.

Blood is thicker than water, so the saying goes. There is comfort and security in that knowledge. But when families are blanketed by silence, blood, water, and heart ties all pour into darkness, as though verbal connections were the very flood walls that had held them together.

Be careful what you do with your silence.

Teach your children to step up and talk when they feel wronged. Let them watch you walk through anger and disappointment, then pick your way back through the words until they arrive at forgiveness, mercy, and connectedness which return the family to being one.

317. DON'T QUIT

I once read a quote that said, "Don't let what you can't do stop you." I typed it up and pasted it on my office wall where I can see it in the midst of my interior and overt struggles. Certainly this wisdom and encouragement applies to parenting, and what a great message to pass along to your kids. It can be demonstrated in a number of ways. When your child just can't figure something out, help them, thereby modeling and expressing that it's okay to seek assistance when they're stumped; let them see you do the same. When your child is frustrated and at the end of their whits, acknowledge the feeling, recalling a similar time in your own life you walked through—then figured out a way or accepted help to conquer.

Seek and share the inspiring lives of others. I've seen stories on television about people who were avid skiers or mountain climbers and then lost their ability to walk. And yet...they adapted a way to hit the slopes or mountains again, even competing. Stevie Wonder, Ray Charles, Andrea Bocelli, all musicians without site who have entertained and inspired us throughout our lives. A single dad, raising a daughter alone, struggling through college on a basketball scholarship. *Victory!* We should be lifted out of our seats by their perseverance and the ability to not let what they couldn't do stop them.

318. GOOD AND EVIL

FEAR

"Warning! warning!" e-mail, TV, and talk radio shows scream. "Trust no one!" "Life stinks!" and on and on. I received one of those warning e-mails that fly around at the speed of light. The scenario covered how bad guys were dressing like policeman and stopping cars. Or, how other bad guys were speeding their cars up next to your car, pointing as though something was wrong, then as

you'd pull over, they'd rob you. This particular writer told her personal story of a person racing up to her car and pointing at something, but she had thankfully just read this article and was wise and so she didn't stop. Lucky for her nothing bad happened. And so we repeat these things to our children, warning that bad guys and gals are everywhere.

I wrote back to everyone on the forwarding list and told my own story. One time, two gentleman raced up to me and pointed to my car. I ignored them, thinking they were flirting. Soon afterwards, I turned a corner and my wallet flew off the roof of my car—where I'd set it after getting a McDonald's burger (which I was cramming down my throat). The wallet hurled across two lanes of speeding traffic.

I also told them about the time a guy raced up next to me and began pointing. I tried to ignore him, thinking he was flirting. (Okay, do we see a mid-life woman here actually hoping someone might still flirt?) He kept insistently motioning for me to roll my window down and I finally did. He hollered that my brakes were smoking and told me to drive to a gas station. I looked in my rear view mirror and saw smoke. I hollered I didn't know where there was a station in that area and he pulled across in front of me, motioned for me to follow him and I did, right to a station—where the gas guy examined my situation and told me I was a hair's breath away from having no brakes. I was one mile from getting on a toll road! I told my children about this.

Stranger? Danger? Angel? Alert yourselves and your children to the fact that random acts of kindness still happen. Not everyone is out to get us. Tell your children about the good guys.

319. Keep it simple

Why, I wonder, are books like *All I Really Need to Know I Learned in Kindergarten* so popular? Because they cut to the heart of what matters without all the big words that take a plethora of psychologists to figure out.

Talk simple. Be simple. Love simple. Your kids will get that message. Hey, we did—it's just that after so many years we forget.

It's time to go back to kindergarten ourselves so we can be reprogrammed to remember that every moment of life doesn't have to be complicated.

320. Recycling

For several years, I volunteered in a resale shop. Proceeds from the shop went to an organization I felt very good about supporting. One of the things I learned from volunteering in that little shop was that it cost me money! There was hardly ever a month when I didn't leave with some treasures. Oh sure, I'd often drop things off when I went. But like the law of supply and demand, my house just seemed to demand to be filled in where it perceived there'd been extractions. A lot of what I brought home was clothing for my boys. I'd find jeans—worn just right—for two bucks. Or t-shirts with funny sayings or like-new winter coats. I often decked myself out as well. Occasionally I'd get the boys to the store with me. Without preaching (which, by the way, I'm very good at) they learned that everything doesn't have to be new to be useful or cool. Yes, I did bring home a few "groaners." But for the most part, we all benefitted and they learned something about the benefits of recycling in an up close and personal way.

321. Stuff happens

Things happen to us: People move away, we move, someone dies, someone graduates, and so on. We're all going so fast these days that we barely take time to mark a notch on our emotional holsters. Pent up batches of loose ends swarm like a writhing snake pit in our heads and hearts. We wonder why we feel so detached, sad, or lonely and then it dawns on us: people move away from our lives and we just keep moving without saying good-bye. Our children, unfortunately, are often too young to have the capacity to sort out these emotions. They just get depressed, just as we do when we don't take time to realize: Something big has happened to us!

Take time for closure. Take time to let it sink in that things happen to you. Things happen to your children. Teach them how to say goodbye and encourage them in new beginnings. Talk about the episodes of your lives and all the emotions that swarm around them.

322. THE HUDDLE

We see it on TV in sporting events: Grown men in tight circles, whispering instructions and encouragement to one another. We just know something important is happening in that little circle, or is about to. Wouldn't it be wonderful if we saw this in homes? Families in tight circles, whispering instructions and encouragement to one another? Perhaps even huddled?

323. MEAN WHAT YOU SAY

Let your "yes" be a yes and your "no" be a no. Kids feel more secure when they know they can count on your final answer, even though they might whine about it for a year. But always remember, you can change your final answer. Just don't do it because they're whining, lest you teach them that whining pays.

324. JUST CHECKING

I used to hate it when my parents would insist on talking to one of my friend's parents, just to make sure things were as we'd stated they were going to be. My kids hated it when I did the same. Nevertheless, my folks did it, I did it, and I bet my kids will one day make those same parental calls. Things *aren't* always as they appear or as our kids state they're going to be. Sometimes they're the last to find out...right after we do. Better to have the little darlings grumbling than to be caught in a situation they're not prepared for. Those will come often enough, even without the calls or warnings. No sense helping them walk through the doors of danger (not to mention wild, unchaperoned parties) just because you didn't make a call or were unwilling to face the momentary sour face of your own kid.

325. Imagine a buck's worth

(Provided by Tina Harrell)

> *Big lessons often arrive in mysterious ways. Take advantage of them when they do.*

Not long before Christmas I went into one of our small town's dollar stores for Christmas gifts. While browsing around, I found a book that had 365 days of single-page Bible stories in it. They were all illustrated and written in a manner that the kids could understand. I was going to give it to my sons as a Christmas gift but just couldn't wait. I gave it to them that evening. They were so excited that they wanted me to start reading right away.

Now every evening while they are all snuggled up in there beds, we spend some "quality time" together and learn about the Bible. It couldn't get any better than that! I was amazed at what one dollar could do for myself and my children's relationship as well as our growth together in faith.

326. Resolving the issues

FEAR

Violence. Gangs. Kids punching each others lights out—sometimes forever. What can a parent do without becoming over protective and isolating them from the joys of life? How can a parent feel they've done all they can to keep their own child from becoming a perpetrator?

One thing we can do is to teach them conflict resolution and appropriate ways to discourse. Watch for classes on this topic and take them together; maybe you could use a few pointers in this arena yourself. Get books on the topic. Tell them that conflict resolution is important! But, most importantly, model resolution rather than rivalry and riff, especially between you and them. When you are knocking heads with your kids (not literally, I hope) calm down, back off, and state a time to come back to the table when tempers have cooled. Talk about how the fact that escalating arguments doesn't solve them. That clarity comes in calm. That louder isn't clearer or more powerful—it's just louder.

327. Sweet mysteries of life

(Provided by Carolyn Armistead)

When I was a little girl, my parents used to take my brother and me on "mystery rides." We would all pile into the car, destination unknown, and try to guess where the trip would take us. Invariably, it would be someplace fun: The ice cream shop, for soft-serve. The playground at sunset. Dinner at a favorite restaurant. Bowling. To the river to feed the ducks.

They were pleasant little outings that were made more special simply by adding an element of mystery and surprise.

328. Inclusion

It's easy to be so involved with our own religious traditions and ethnic origins that we send a subtle message to our children that we're White, African American, Asian, Hispanic, Muslim, Protestant, Catholic, Jewish, etc....and that is all that matters. Find books on your child's level about other nationalities, customs, and locations. Teach them to honor, seek, and respect those who are not exactly like them. Don't propagate prejudices; work deliberately and overtly against them. Let your children hear you speak up against injustice and bigoted opinions.

Perhaps a community college or other civic organization hosts cultural events; attend them together. A natural opportunity to focus on other ethnic groups is to study them before upcoming holidays: Chinese New Year and Ramadan, Hanukkah and Christmas. Expand your child's vision of the world; after all, they are the next generation and they'll one day be running it.

329. Bulbs of faith

(Provided by Tena DeGraaf)

From botanist to zoologist, like Tena says, working with your child brings opportunities for more than you might imagine.

❧❧

On a crisp October morning, my sons and I emerged from the garage holding gardening equipment: one small shovel, 60 tulip bulbs, bone meal, a sand shovel, and a clear plastic bug box. We progressed to the circle of mulch surrounding the ash tree in our front yard. Tasks were divided in our small group of garden enthusiasts. I dug the 6 inch holes and added the bone meal. Daniel, age 3, put the tulip bulb right side up. Mitchell, age 2, got to cover the flower bulb with his plastic shovel.

Every once in a while I would uncover a worm when digging, and we would switch from botanists to zoologists by putting the worms into the bug box for observation. At one point during this procedure Daniel stated confidently, "You know Mom, God makes the worms, too!" I smiled and replied, "Yes, He does." The remainder of the morning was spent working together and continuing our discussion of God's creations. I look forward to each March when the tulips bloom because they not only represent the "flowers" of our labor, but they symbolize the seeds of faith planted that morning.

330. Eat it up

The U.S. Department of Agriculture has come up with something to help us teach our kids about nutrition: a food guide pyramid for young children. Geared toward kids 2- to 6-years-old, it can help them (and us) understand what the heck we're babbling on about when we talk about food groups. It works because it speaks their (my) language in visuals. Rather than just saying a word such as fat, it shows a stick of butter and a lollipop at the top of that pyramid. (It's a teeny, tiny point. Argh.) You can either download this pyramid from their Web site (*www.usda.gov/cnpp*) or order one for five bucks from the USDA.

But wait, that's not all: If you are Web savvy, you and your child can visit the site, log in, type in everything you ate for a day and actually receive a dietary assessment. Yikes!

Tackle health issues together. Put that pyramid on your fridge door and hold each other accountable. The good news is (at least for me): waffles and spaghetti and bread have the largest slot.

331. A GOOD FOUNDATION

Ask a trusted friend who is often privy to your family what they admire about the relationship between you and your child. You might be surprised; you might be affirmed. Either way, it's good to build on our strengths because we waste enough time fretting about our weaknesses.

332. THE WAY TO A CHILD'S HEART

(Provided by Barbara Kauffman)

Recognize and celebrate events in your child's life, even the seemingly little occurrences. And what better way than by giving them an edible smile to put on their breakfast, lunch, or dinner plate. It's also a great after-school or work snack. Any age through adulthood would appreciate such fun recognition. Here's how you do it:

Use an apple wedger on a large red apple. Take two of the wedges and smear inside edges with creamy peanut butter. Lay one wedge on a plate with peanut butter face-up. Set miniature marshmallows on end all along the outward curved edge of the apple. Place the remaining wedge, peanut butter side down, on top the marshmallows to create a pair of smiling red lips with a toothy grin! The note you put at their place could say, "You make me smile when/because you _____." Fill in the blank with a behavior, attitude, or action you observed and want to recognize and celebrate. If it happens to be for someone who is in the loose baby-tooth stage of life, be sure and leave out a couple of marsh-mallows to represent the missing teeth!

333. The art of perseverance

Because I'm an author, I love hearing stories about best-selling books and movies that were rejected by 37 publishers and/or producers before they hit the big time. What an encouragement, inspiration, and incentive to chase your dream with a spirit of relentless pursuit. But first, sentence by sentence, word by word, they had to write the piece (or fill in the blank) then believe in it enough to never give up. Much like the Little Engine that Could, it first had to think so.

From tying their shoes, to playing the piano, to making the team, to doing 10 sit ups to whatever they need or desire to master, help your child establish goals in manageable chunks so they don't become discouraged and give up when the first baby step doesn't lead to success. Have them name the goal, define it clearly, and figure out what would be the first step in moving toward it. What's the second? What's the third? Make a chart or graph. Let them know everyone has a few missed steps along the way when they blow it. And if the steps just don't seem to be achievable, help them reevaluate the goal. Was it reasonable? Doable? Worth it? Have they discovered something else along the way that interests them more?

Whether they achieve the goal or not, your faith and assistance in helping them move toward it will be remembered for a lifetime.

334. Questions? I've got questions

In a book titled *Dangerous Wonder*, author Mike Yaconelli says, "When parents understand their role, they understand that they do not exist to answer every question their children have. Parents must help children discern the *important* questions, the life-giving questions." He sites examples of these as, "What is my calling? Where do I find meaning? Where does forgiveness come from? How do I serve others? How can I learn how to love my enemies?"

Helping your child find the important questions will also help them realize which ones don't really matter in the grand scheme of things, and who among us couldn't use a little more training in *that?*

335. THE GOOD CHILD

Kids with special needs need special attention, no way around it. Kids who get in trouble need special attention, no doubt about it. Kids who are in a "good child" spell (or were seemingly born that way) need attention too, lest they become the "needy one" just to get attention or become the "lost one" because, well, they *were* lost within their own family.

Notice the good child. Hug the good child. Pay close attention to the good child. Sometimes they're lonely, troubled, or just better at covering up or not rocking the boat. But always, they seem to get less attention than the other one. Can we see the problem here?

336. THREE'S JUST RIGHT

Every once in a while it's wonderful to be able get to out to lunch or dinner (or breakfast or snacks, for that matter) with your friends. No kids. Just grown-up talk.

On occasion, however, it is an act of honor to invite your child along. Let them witness you enjoying your friendships, validating the importance of relationships. Maybe let them overhear you telling your friend about one of their achievements or how proud of them you are, just for being who they are.

At the same time you also validate your child's importance: They are as esteemed as your friends.

337. PAINS THAT PASS

I recently spoke at a parenting event that was for mothers of multiple births. My favorite part of their evening (aside from me, of course...just kidding) was when they had the opportunity to voice a parental problem they were encountering. All the moms were given the chance to supply a solution. If they couldn't provide a solution, they could at least provide a group moan of sympathy.

One of the moms said one of her twins was biting. No matter what she did—biting him back, the time-out chair, other discipline—he wouldn't stop. This was one of those big group moans. Biting is a difficult phase to apprehend.

When I took the podium afterwards, here was my insight: "My boys are now 35 and 29 and I'm happy to report that neither of them are still biting." Of course this wasn't a whole lot of consolation for the ones receiving the bites, but everyone laughed, hope was given, and a glimpse of the light at the end of the tunnel served as a balm for the wearied and worried parental warrior. Sometimes laughter alone can do that, along with the simple reminder that this, too, shall pass.

(However, if you happen to know my sons and realize that I'm the last person to know that they are still biting, don't tell me, okay?)

338. CUTTING A PATH

Out our living room window and kitty-cornered from our yard I can see something beautiful: A dad is mowing the lawn; his preschooler son is also mowing, just like dad. Of course dad's lawnmower is powerful and loud and actually cuts a path. The preschooler's mower is bright red and yellow and plastic and cuts nothing. But there is something—in the midst of all that cutting—that is blossoming between these two mower men. I can see it.

Allow your child the privilege of working with you, even if what they're "doing" isn't quite doing anything, other than the fact that they're doing it with you.

Yes, I can see that the mower men are now cutting a path toward each other. I can see it.

339. MORNING MUSIC

I read an article that recommended everyone—every one—in a family should occasionally sing their words before breakfast. No speaking; just singing.

Sometimes the morning chaos does lend itself to tense, cranky, and frenzied moments. Perhaps singing our words would not only add a little levity but make even those moments a bit easier to take when all you can think is: "She's not out of the bathroom yet! Did you pack your lunch? Get out of bed now!"

340. REVELATIONS

One Sunday, we went to visit my husband's mom and dad. When we arrived, my husband went through familiar greetings, then he went into the living room, plopped down (and I do mean plopped) into a chair, turned sideways and flipped his legs over one of the arms to watch television. I sat there staring at him, mouth agape, for I'd never seem him do this before. Ever. Obviously it was something he'd done many times before in this setting, in this house, in this chair, in his youth. I didn't say a word; I just sat studying, taking in this endearing sliver of a glimpse of my fifty-something, 6'2" husband as a child.

The older, and sometimes mouthier our children get, the easier it is to lose sight of the fact that standing before us is the same child whom we cuddled and coddled and who grinned us that adorable toothless and drooling grin. And yes, that adorable one still lives within this "wretched one" before us whose gangly body and awkward gate and sassiness drives us to the brink.

Watch for evidence of that adorable one. It helps to be reminded that they still live. (This includes spouses and significant others, as well.)

341. INVESTMENTS

In 1996, I was a Celebrity Judge for White Castle Hamburger's Fifth Annual Cravetime Recipe Contest. (For those of you who don't know what a White Castle Hamburger is, I'm taking a moment to feel sorry for you.) Because our entire family loves these tiny, steamed burgers with holes in the patty meat, when I told my grown sons about this, they both immediately vowed they were going to come to Ohio for the festivities. (I think they secretly hoped they'd get lots of free stuff but I didn't let on I knew that.) And so they did. My men children, watching mom do her thing. Cheering me on. Payback, if you will, for all the years I seasoned my own bleacher buns cheering for them. Return on the investment. Investments in one another that keep us connected.

What was, or will be, your deposit today?

342. TALK TO THE BAG

Whining kids can make you want to disconnect from parenthood about as quickly as anything. "But *Moooooom.*" "*Daaaaaad*, you never let me ..." "I waaaaaaant to." That pitch is way up there on the scale, and its reach is way down there into our gut. Its effect goes right to our brain. Our mouths that begin to operate on their own by screaming things like "Be quiet before I do something terrible!"

Be of good cheer! I've just learned about something that is brilliant and I'm going to stop typing right now and try it on George. (Just kidding, he doesn't whine; I do.) I heard of a mom who tells her kid that she doesn't have time to listen to his whining at the moment and that he should whine into the paper bag she then hands him. When he's done whining—which of course he can barely continue to do without laughing—she seals it and tells him she'll listen to it later.

Although my baby is already a mid-lifer and I don't have a chance to test this on a young one, it feels inspired. (I might try this with myself some day before George gets home so he doesn't have to listen to me.) It is also symbolic of how we can rise to the occasion with humor if we put our minds and creativity to it.

343. CREATION

Declare a period of time (15 minutes to an hour) in which each person in your family needs to create something. A poem, a watercolor, origami, an amazing salad, a tower of cards, a song on your clarinet, a swimming pool for worms (I don't recommend this), a demonstration of Cub Scout knots, a pulled-together fashion statement—anything. Set the timer and then reconvene around the kitchen table with your creations when it goes off. One by one, display, play, demonstrate, and read your creations.

Then, have each person write down one word that describes their creative entry, put them in a hat (or whatever) and have everyone draw from the pile. If you get your own, you have to put it back and draw another one. Set the timer again and each person now dispatches again to work at their newly assigned creation task. This gives everyone the chance to appreciate what talents their mom or dad, child or sibling has as they try to walk a bit in their shoes.

Appreciation for one another is a great thing to learn and teach. This is a simple, tangible way to begin to understand the concept—for everyone.

344. YOUR OWN SHADOW

GROUNDHOG DAY

Put a new spin on Groundhog Day. Rather than wait to hear what the Master Guru Rodent sees or doesn't see, have each person in your household, one at a time, look in the mirror and tell what they see in their future for the next year—aside from a haircut, the removal of braces, or more wrinkle cream.

345. OUR OWN BACKYARDS

We met some friends of ours when they moved next door to us from the East coast. They lived in our area nearly a decade and then they moved back east. The funniest thing was to hear them talk about returning to Chicago for a visit afterwards so they could see all the sights and museums they never saw when they lived here.

My kids most often saw those types of things when out-of-towners came who wanted to see the Museum of Science and Industry and Shedd Aquarium. The visitors had read about all kinds of things in preparation for their vacation that half the time we'd never heard about having lived here our entire lives.

Be an explorer in your own area. Get yourself brochures from nearby chambers of commerce and your state. Vacation in your own area like you've never seen it before because you probably haven't; at least not through the fresh and curious eyes of a visitor.

346. Blow me a kiss

When I was a Den Mother, one of my favorite projects we ever endeavored was making special Father's Day hankies for the dads. We pinned hankies over large pieces of cardboard to hold them taught. Each child then drew their sentiments or art work on the hanky with crayons. We moved the finished object between two pieces of brown paper bag and slowly ironed the hanky, which melted the crayon markings into the fabric, dying in the patterns.

Cotton hankies are easy to take with you, stuffed in a handbag, lunch box, back pocket, briefcase, backpack, worn as a headband, tied on a bike handle, whatever. Dedicate a hanky to each family member and have everyone add their unique thought or object. This way, when Mom or Dad is on the road, Sis or Brother is away at camp, or you're all just heading to wherever, your "Love Hanky" can become a take-away reminder for him or her to physically take away pieces of personal love.

On rocky days when it just feels like a good idea to remind everyone that they do love each other, embark in a ceremony to tie your hankies all together as a symbol of your family's unity.

347. SHOW TIME!

I recall a few occasions growing up when my brother and I gathered all our friends to put on a play. We'd follow a known storyline sometimes, but more often we'd make up our own drama. We'd use a clothesline and sheet for the curtain and raid our closets and dress-up boxes for costumes. All the neighborhood kids became actors and actresses. Those who didn't want to be in the play would operate the curtain, set up chairs, and con their parents out of snacks to make a refreshment stand. We actually charged our parents to come watch us; I believe we got a quarter a piece.

The thing I remember about these is how excited my mom always acted as she awaited showtime. She'd holler down in the basement every 15 minutes or so to see if it was time yet. Each inquiry let us know she was thinking about us, planning on attending, and truly looking forward to our production. She believed in it.

Sure, it's fun to encourage your kids to put on a play. It would even be fun to suggest having your entire family be involved in a production for the neighborhood. But most importantly, I want to pass along how wonderful my mom's enthusiasm made me feel and how I appreciated and loved her so for it. I still do.

348. AN EXCUSE TO CELEBRATE

(Provided by Carolyn Armistead)

Celebrate half-birthdays; everybody's half-birthdays—moms, grandparents, kids, dogs, cats. It's easy and fun. The one celebrating a half-birthday chooses the dinner menu, and may get a small gift or card to mark the day. A half-cupcake with a half-candle in it, and a rousing chorus of "Happy Half-Birthday To You" are also fun.

349. IT'S ALL RELATIVE

I'm sure I learned something about Albert Einstein when I was in school but all that seemed to stick was that he was very smart and had wild hair. Recently, however, I've run across several quotes that really inspired me to learn more about him and so I purchased a book on this relativity guy. Had I not accidentally and absent-mindedly left the book in an airport, I'd probably know even more. Anyhow, here's some of my favorite quotes of his, which will lead me to my point:

> *"I have no particular talent; I am merely inquisitive."*
>
> *"When I examined myself and my methods of thought, I came to the conclusion that the gift of fantasy has meant more to me than my talent for absorbing positive knowledge."*

Keep these things in mind as you decide how to go about inspiring your child. All the right classes, grades, and colleges cannot make up for one's ability and desire to "find out." To let their imaginations run wild. Now that's something to spend a moment pondering—and in my case celebrating!

350. Eye of the Beholder

At the reception of the remarriage of a friend of mine, her grandchildren were racing around with disposable cameras, capturing those amazing, knee-capped moments. It was toward the end of the evening and they looked like busy little boys after a few hours at a dress-up occasion: wonderfully disheveled! Shirt tails were hanging, hair was askew, shoes were off... Oh how I adore recollections of my own boys appearing before me in that special way. Real-life, fun-induced disheveled moments and memories are much more precious to me than when they're all niced up, stiff, and grinning.

Alex, the younger brother, came my way and I squatted down to give him a bear hug. About that time his older brother Stephen entered the room. "Look Stephen," I said. "Here's a photo opportunity for you." I drew Alex as close as could be and together we grinned at the photographer. He drew up his camera, aimed for a spell, then let the hand with the camera drop to his side. In a dramatic (albeit momentary) gesture, he announced, "Waste of film!" He spun on his heels and departed around the corner to rejoin the rest of the party.

The moral of this story: Some moments are more important to *be* in than to waste time capturing. Remember this the next time you are fervently witnessing life through the camera lens during an important occasion, rather than taking in all of life around it.

351. WHAT WE SAY

Children can be so cruel to one another, and I mean *cruel.* They may be cruel physically, but verbally they can humiliate, slice and dice, embarrass, and harass. And don't think *your* child isn't capable of it. You'd be amazed what your own child can do (I know I certainly was). If your children need attention or feel like they're not powerful enough in the food chain, they'll rank on someone else. (Come to think about it, I'm amazed how awful I can be sometimes!)

When you hear your child, or the kids they're playing with, talk poorly to another. Or, if you hear them making fun of "fatso," "geek," "dork," or "ugly," even if the other child isn't around, do something. Intervene. Let them know talking poorly about others is not acceptable. Tell them it's cruel and that they need to consider the hearts of others. But make sure to listen to yourself as well. Gossip and mean talk—even if it is about your boss or your jerk of a co-worker—are both taught by example.

352. HAPPY TO SEE YOU

My husband, a 6'2" strapping and sturdy guy, completely revealed his tenderest heart as he talked about how he used to sit on the front porch of their bungalow and wait for his father to arrive home from work every night. "He'd be so happy," George said, "to see me sitting there, waiting for him." The sparkle in George's eyes as he talked about the joy in his father's eyes was brilliant.

"If he didn't have his paper yet, he'd give me a buck and I'd run to the store and get him one. He always let me keep the change. That's how I collected that big bottle of change I've had since we've been married."

Oh how many wonderful things happened in this daily ritual of a dad being happy to see a waiting son: joy, connectedness, warmth, memories...and money. Now that's a hard-to-beat combination!

353. RESERVATIONS FOR TWO

(Provided by Karin Baker)

I was right out of college when my father got his calling into the ministry. I was moving back home so that I could save money for my wedding and mom and dad where moving to another state. I felt alone and wondered what I was going to do without my parents.

That following week, my grandfather Earl and I went to dinner together just for each other's company. We had a really good time just talking about our lives. We were talking about how different we are and how alike we can be as well. These dinners became a weekly event and we looked forward to getting together just to relax and talk.

Through the years, the dinners have turned into lunches. We also added going to church together on Sundays. My grandfather has been a big part of my life and the raising of my children because we always have at least this one hour in the middle of a week just to talk.

Our weekly lunches are known by all we encounter. My co-workers call me and say, "Hey Karin, your grandpa is outside waiting for you." Our family members will call and say, "I know you are meeting with Grandpa today; can you say hello for me?" And even the ladies at our lunch spot will see us walk in and say, "Reservations for two coming up." They even know what our normal drink order is and bring it to us before we ask.

The time spent with my grandfather has become as important to me as the time I spend with my children in the evenings after work. Spending time with an older relative can really open your eyes up to how you now deal with situations, as if it were through hereditary. You also learn a lot from their mistakes. Take advantage of the free advice and take time to listen to a grandpa! Maybe you can even make reservations for two!

354. AN UNLIKELY HARVEST

I just received an e-mail from my friend Jane Ruser telling me about their glorious Father's Day weekend. She said they had a very relaxing day—and that they'd even slept in until 10 a.m. However, there was only one interruption at 4:50 a.m. when Monica threw up in her bed, an early Father's Day gift!

She then went on to ask me if she'd told me about the time their son had pee running down his leg in the porta potty. (No, in fact she hadn't. Thankfully.) However, I was suddenly lost in reminiscence of all yucky (yet grace-filled) days gone by: Brian running around the house holding his butt, not wanting to "go" on the toilet so badly that he'd finally hide behind anything to fill his pants; puke running down the back of my good dress from a volcanic burp; and the taste of pee in my mouth from my first little boy diaper-changing learning curve. Priceless moments.

I'm not sure why, but these gross incidents end up held in our hearts as pure, spun gold. Remember that when you're swabbing the decks of your home fronts. Have mercy on those little ones, for they are the ones planting those seeds of gold. Tend kindly to the harvest, folks.

355. MADE WITH LOVE

When my mom died, I think she still had every handmade gift I'd ever given her—from a bar of soap with things stuck in it to quite a lovely sweater I'd crocheted. I've done the same with my kids. I have Brian's handprint in plaster in a bedroom; two necklaces Bret made me out of plaster and strung metal parts in my jewelry box; a clay flower pot with dripping paint that says "mother" and "hi" along with flowers, music notes, hearts, and a cross, each in primary colors, on a shelf; a sign tooled in a shop class that says "#1 Mom" still on display in my kitchen; and more. Although store-bought gifts can be truly wonderful, there is something about a gift of thought and planning, cutting and hammering, stitching and gluing, that arrives blessedly cloaked in the fingerprints of those we love.

No matter how simple (cutting out a paper heart and scribbling on it) or complicated (patterns or drawings and four months to make), encourage and assist your child in creating and giving a gift. Who knows, you might receive the benefits of that investment yourself one day.

356. Doing it one's self

I stopped by my neighbor's house one day and the first thing she said was, "You should see what Natalie's making for dinner!" We scurried into the kitchen where Mom began to stir noodles into boiling water for her daughter. From there on in, however, it was all kid cooking. Before we knew it (other than the spilled milk moment) macaroni and cheese was served up by a grinning girl who'd made supper herself.

Although it's easier to do it yourself, don't always. Instruct. Assist. Encourage. Demonstrate. Help them learn how to clean up their own spills and messes. After all, a skill well taught is one less you'll have to do!

357. The home team

When the boys were growing up, every once in a while we'd take them to a major league ballgame, or the stock car or harness races. Together we'd cheer, hoop, and holler for our favorite team, player, number, or color tail—whatever means we chose to make our selection. Occasionally we weren't even all rooting for the same side, but that was okay too. In fact, it often made it the most lively when we were rooting against one another.

Get involved with something with your children that causes you to cheer! Enthusiasm can carry over into other parts of life. It'll do them good (and hopefully wear them out), let them see the side of you that can occasionally cut lose—and you can usually buy popcorn and all kinds of snacks at about any of these events. For me, that's enough incentive in itself!

358. CONFIDENCE

The voice of confidence—one voice of confidence—can carry us a long way in the midst of our own doubt. I once read a quote that went something like this: "If you can't believe in yourself right now, believe in *my* faith in you." Now that is profound, especially since children are vulnerable and blindly believe what we tell them. (Unless they are teenagers in which case they might believe your word is dirt. Or at least they might act like that.)

When your child is tackling a new endeavor or struggling along with the same one that seems to haunt him or her on a daily basis, be that voice of confidence. No matter how negatively your child might respond, speak confidence anyway.

359. LET IT GO

Holding a grudge can feel good. Really good. After all, that jerk deserves to be ignored. She's not worthy of my forgiveness. If my kid wants to act like *that*...I told them a thousands times to be more careful and *now* look what happened. I am just not getting over it. And I mean it.

Holding a grudge can feel bad. Real bad. I mean stomach troubles, headaches, and tense muscles. Staying angry never closes a gap. Never. If you think one of your kids isn't punished enough for whatever offense (I'm not talking about consequences; I'm talking about your anger), staying mad often doesn't punish the offender. However, it certainly punishes yourself. Anger can make you sick, stifle your judgment, and hurl you into vindictive, juvenile, wounding actions.

I repeat: Staying angry never closes a gap. It spreads wide the jaws of separation and holds them there.

360. THERE AND BACK

We spend so much time shuffling our kids around in the car that it just makes sense to use it for more purposes than getting from here to there. Rather than crank up your favorite radio channel or just succumb to one more round of your child's favorite (albeit irritating) song, have them help you navigate when they get old enough to count streets and/or recognize landmarks—even if you do know where you're going (and since you're driving, I certainly hope you do).

If you have access to the Web, print out portions of maps of your town or neighborhood (or simply draw them), making them large and easy enough for young eyes to follow. Maybe even color in landmarks or have them do so. Then as you're on your journey, have them watch for those landmarks and try to "help" direct you. Who knows, it might entice you into paying more attention to the world around you that otherwise goes mindlessly by. I know I often have moments of wondering how I've arrived someplace. Scary, huh?

361. THE ART OF WORDS

(Provided by Rich Latta)

*There are many ways to speak to your children
about their lives. Find one that comes naturally to you
and begin.*

I have always written poetry. I started writing poems about my daughters concerning things I had watched them accomplish, struggle with, or create. Sometimes I'd write an inspirational poem about how they shouldn't let life frustrate them. They were all done in free verse. I usually spent the most time writing them in November to December to put in their stockings on Christmas

Eve. It was amazing to watch them run to the stockings and sit and read those poems before even looking for the goodies or small gifts. My wife would let them read them for a day or two then she put them in a binder.

When the oldest daughter got married, my wife gave them to her on her wedding day. I was even amazed to see the volume of poems I had written. It was a fascinating record of her life growing up and what I had observed in that life. My other younger daughters also got to glimpse at their volumes. Their poetry volumes will be given to them at some appropriate time.

362. WORDS OF WISDOM

(Provided by Sheri Schubbe)

I love to connect with my children at the local public library! My two children (ages 4 and 2 1/2) have been visiting the library on a weekly basis for two years. We love to select great stories, as well as nonfiction children's books on animals, tractors, and whatever else. After we choose the kids' books, we ride in the elevator upstairs to the "Mommy Section" and pick out a book for me!

Both of my children know library etiquette and how to check out a book. But the best part is when we snuggle on the couch throughout the week and read our books together. I truly feel that my children are developing a love of learning and books from our weekly library visits, and hope that they will always remember our reading time together.

363. GRIPPED

After my father died and before my son knew Dad's wishes were to be cremated, my grown son, in his grief and pain, stated how we needed to make sure Grandpa's hands were showing in the casket. My dad had uniquely shaped hands, his fingers having taken all kinds of beatings from semi-pro baseball, his tool and die trade, not to mention the battle wounds of other miscellaneous "manly" projects throughout his life. My dad's hands were unique.

But most importantly, my dad's hands were available. He was a hands-on dad and grandpa who used his warm palms to hug us, build whatever needed building, teach us how to cast a fishing line, hold the reins of a racehorse as we cheered him on at the track, cut the watermelon on our picnics, or whatever else we needed.

Dad's hands were available. Are yours?

364. Downhill from here

On a visit to my son's, I watched him ride away from me on his Gold Wing motorcycle, disappearing down the big hill in front of his home, waving over his shoulder. (This was the youngest child; the oldest would be careening on his Harley Davidson.) He was on his way to work, but so many visions of yesteryear flashed through my mind that I could barely slow them down enough to flip through them one at a time: My sons, down the slide, arms "dangerously" outstretched over their heads; down the sledding hill, snowsuited and looking like exploded cotton balls; down the road, in their first car; down the stairs, wearing a Cub Scout uniform; down the ski slopes, grown, fearless and flying...

See child grin. See child walk. See child run. See child go, go, go, go.

See child while you can. They are quickly going down the hill, into life without you. But do not waste time thinking about that. With all that's in you, watch them climb, climb...

365. The bottom line

My massage therapist is a gifted and thoughtful woman who applies her talents to her life and her job. (I am one of the many who blissfully reaps the benefits.) Throughout the course of my visits we have touched upon the topic of parenting. (This is, of course, before I am totally turned to sponge.) Jane speaks very lovingly about her mom and her mom's poignant role in her life. She specifically shared one special gift her mom has given her:

Her mom has always encouraged Jane to find *her own* answers. Jane said her mom doesn't leave her hanging, but she supports her in finding her own way. "She realized *she* didn't have *my* answers," Jane says, "but she'll offer suggestions. My mom's genuine interest and unconditional love helped me find the answers from within myself."

For instance, as Jane searched to discover her vocational path, it was always obvious she was, to put it in her words, "a caretaker type of person." There were those who heartily encouraged and told her to go into nursing. Somehow Jane just knew—although she didn't know why—it wasn't the right path for her. She talked about how her mom just encouraged her to be herself. How she was as a person in whatever course she chose was more important than what she did.

Eventually Jane came to massage therapy. (Thanks Jane's mom, from me!) Jane says, "I'm grateful for her assistance in my enlightenment." Jane is referring to much more than her choice in vocation—she's referring to her entire approach to life.

What a testimony this is to a parent who not only knew how to connect with the very heart and essence of her child, but who honorably tutored her child in connecting with the inner most bright and trustworthy places in herself.

In Closing...

I hope the last entry in this book (Number 365: The bottom line) doesn't feel like a closing at all. But that it—much like all the entries that preceded it—renders inspiration and hope for the days to come. May they bring you joy during days of discovery, anticipation, encouragement, discouragement, and bliss. May they bring you joy durin days of capitulating, celebrating, contemplating, and adulating. All roads will lead to joyful connectedness if you, with humility and honor, stand upon a solid commitment to succeed at arriving there. Although all parents have their regrets, staying connected with your children will never be one of them. May you live in the grace, grit, and glory of succeeding.

INDEX

ABOUT THE AUTHOR

Charlene Ann Baumbich is a Child of God, woman, wife, mom, author, speaker, and humorist who writes and talks about the layers of life, whether they're good, bad, or dubious. She's also lots of other things on any given day (and some of them aren't pretty); just ask her husband, kids, friends, neighbors, and sometimes complete strangers.

For those of you who "do" computer: Drop by her Web site at *www.dontmissyourlife.com* to find out where she'll be appearing next, as well as to review a list of her books and speaking topics, just in case you'd like to inquire about having her come entertain, inspire, and rejuvinate your group. You can also sign up right from the Web site (and isn't *that* slick?!) to be on her mailing list, wherein she will notify you a few times of year about new column posts, book releases, and her birthday.

While you're visiting *www.dontmissyourlife.com*, make sure you check out "Words to Help You Twinkle," her Web column (sifted through no editors so she can ramble on about anything she likes, misspellings all the while) along with her *very* perky photo!

E-mail: *charlene@dontmissyourlife.com*